BEST GAY EROTICA 1999

Richard Labonté, Series Editor

Selected and introduced by Felice Picano

BEST GAY EROTICA 1999

Richard Labonté, Series Editor

Selected and introduced by Felice Picano

CLEIS PRESS

Published in the United States by Cleis Press Inc., P.O. Box 14684, San Francisco, California 94114.
Printed in the United States.
Cover design: Scott Idleman
Text design: Frank Wiedemann
Cleis logo art: Juana Alicia
First Edition.
10 9 8 7 6 5 4 3 2 1

Contents

for Asa Dean Liles, my anchor

to Katherine Forrest & Jo Hurcus & Michael Nava, with love

for Lawrence Schimel, my friend

Foreword
Richard Labonté

Editing this fourth edition of *Best Gay Erotica* (my third) provided me with a kind of epiphany: as we go into 1999, the amount of porn in circulation is a manifold multiple of what it was even five years ago.

As a bookseller, I've been conscious of the greater number of erotic-toned tomes from a growing number of publishers—from venerable Leyland Publications, of course, and more recently Masquerade/Badboy; mainstream Plume's *Flesh and the Word* series and the newer *Friction* series from Alyson Publications; the *Quickies* series from Arsenal Pulp, the specialized genre-erotica of Circlet Press, the every-two-months-pace of John Patrick's Starbooks, a *Mammoth Book of Gay Erotica* from England, the porn novels of Prowler Press and Idol/Virgin, and even erotic collections from Painted Leaf in New York, which began business just a couple of years ago publishing some excellent poetry collections.

There continue to be the dozens of glossy men's magazines—*In Touch* and *Indulge* and *Torso* and *Advocate Men* and *Freshmen* and *Mandate*, and the less glossy *Bear* and *Bulk Male*, *Chiron Rising* and *Men in Uniform*, *Cowpoke* and *GBM* (Gay Black Male), a wide range of arousing writing (and images) which, for many a gay man, are his first exposure to "gay" and "writing."

So there is plenty of in-print *Best* potential to consider—no surprise, since writing about sex, and reading writing about sex, and having sex while reading writing about sex (often but not always alone), are elemental to the human experience (those fundies aside).

I tapped into those books and skimmed those magazines last year and the year before that, looking for candidates for my first two *Best Gay* collections to supplement and complement those brought in by the standard call for submissions. I narrowed a couple of hundred down to a few dozen, and then the judges (Douglas Sadownick, Christopher Bram) picked twenty or so winners.

What was different this year? I logged on to the Internet (probably a couple of years after I should have).

The number of stories I read in 1998 for this 1999 edition exploded—from that couple of hundred to way more than a thousand.

I scoured the excellent *Blithe House Quarterly* fiction website, where I found one author for this edition (Lawrence Ytzhak Braithwaite); I scrolled through hundreds and hundreds of stories at gay.net, at *The Gay Cafe/Nifty Erotic Stories Archive*, at *Night Charm*, at *Mature Fur*, at *Gayscape*, at *Ben Boxer's Clubhouse*, at dozens more sites, at one of which I found Dan Taulapapa McMullin's story; I read through wrestling fetish pages and spanking fetish pages and muscle fetish pages and tickling fetish pages and piss fetish pages and college-boy fetish pages and jack-off fetish pages and cigar fetish pages and underwear fetish pages and foot fetish pages and butt fetish pages...one link leading to ten more and each of those to dozens more, with not that much overlap. One particularly worthy site was Gary Bowen's *Roughriders*, where transgender sex is the motif, destined to be a source for this anthology sometime.

In the end, I found a lot of raw first-person narrative porn, cliché-ridden and linguistically stunted but passionate and immediate (*"I was real horny when I got up but I had to go piss before I could pull my boner and oh boy I was glad I did because the furry silver-haired Asian fitness trainer across from my bathroom window with the dollar-sized pierced nipples and buzzcut was already standing stark naked in his bedroom working out those big tattooed muscles of his with his horsecock dangling through the bottom of his skintight swimsuit and when he saw me staring at him he winked and I almost creamed while I was pissing,"* for example). Anyone with a modem can post such stories, anyone else with both a modem and a printer can take them to bed (which touches on the topic of the erotic tactility of reading explored by 1999 judge Felice Picano in his introduction).

It's a return to the sort of to-the-point wish fulfillment "I"-person prose collated and honored (and edited with care) by the late Boyd McDonald in *Straight to Hell/STH: The "Manhattan Review of Unnatural Acts,"* and in his early collections *Meat*, *Sex*, *Flesh*, *Cum*, *Wads*, *Juice*, *Filth* and a couple of others I've forgotten, often imitated but never equaled—though the webworld of unfiltered prose porn is cumming on strong.

And, in truth, the masturbatory image quoted above (actually cobbled together from a handful of postings) shares the turn-on of voyeurism of Michael Lassell's contribution this year; the difference between what's basic and what's *Best* stems from Lassell's technical skill, not his intent. That intent—to write about what thrills sexually—is the simple common denominator shared by both the winners in *Best Gay Erotica 1999* and those boys and men with their modems and their imaginations. Some of it is good writing by subjective standards and all of it is erotic writing by someone's standards (if only the author's), whether it is read in this anthology or posted as a single Web page at a hard-to-find URL.

As usual, the winners are a varied lot; there are contributors with multiple appearances, such as Jameson Currier (four of four), Lassell and Simon Shepphard (three of four), Kelly McQuain and horehound stillpoint (two of four). Currier's is an edgy story of chance lust, Lassell's a ribald story of sustained lust, Sheppard's a grinning story of mechanical lust, McQuain's a complex story of anguished lust and stillpoint's a fevered story of ecstatic lust.

The power in sex of one man over another is a theme common to three very different stories: Jeff Kirby's "Puppy Love," about the pleasure of role-playing; Ian Phillips' "See Dick Deconstruct," a wicked mix of queer theory and passionate practice; and the all-too-brief excerpt from Larry Townsend's gripping novel *A Contagious Evil: The Mind of a Serial Killer,* one of judge Picano's top five picks, about the barriers between lust and death, between intelligence and insanity, and what happens when those barriers break down.

Memory is the motif for "Body Hunger" by Grigoris Daskalogrigorakis, whose narrator culls incidents, moments, and images from his past, for present pleasure; and in a different way memory is the theme for "Yellow" by Kirk Read, whose narrator returns to his boyhood home and his older brother; and different again for "Six Positions" by Andy Quan, whose narrator brings the sense of sex with others into his own sensual moment.

Three of the stories this year are sardonic erotic commentaries on gay male desire. Jim Coughenour's "Castro: A Manifesto" is, indeed, a manifesto on posing and pretense; and Dan Taulapapa McMullin's "Unsafe Cyber" is wry writing on what's true and what's false online. And though there are playful elements in most of the stories I've mentioned, Belasco's comic-strip "Sixteen Degrees of Penetration" most made me smile; without words, Belasco conveys the joyous release of damn good sex.

My editor's choice this year is Lawrence Ytzhak Braithwaite's novel excerpt, "A New Harrington and Oxblood Rules, o.k. (Jumping the Broom)," a subtle evocation of desire between young men played out above the waist and in their minds, in a milieu where it's not easy for men to love men. Braithwaite, author of the novel *Wigger*, writes with a vernacular passion at first tricky to take in, until it clicks—try reading it aloud.

Thanks go this year to editors Alan Mills, Lawrence Schimel, and James Johnstone for "nominating" work for consideration; and once again to Ken White at A Different Light in San Francisco, for juggling the manuscript mail while I traveled, and to Tommi Avicolli Mecca, also of ADL/SF, for transmuting an array of emails and email attachments and word processing programs and PC/Mac confrontations into the simple elderly WordPerfect program I can actually use; and to Frédérique Delacoste, Felice Newman, and Don Weise at Cleis Press, comfortable folks with whom to work.

The Many Erotics of Reading: Introduction

Felice Picano

At a literary conference several years ago, I found myself seated on one of those reiterating panels, faced with the reiterating problem of determining exactly what was erotic and what was pornographic, and whether the two could ever be completely separated in our literary culture, or whether they were somehow inextricably bound together.

For my own self the answer was no—and yes. I knew how I myself differentiated the two: pornography had one purpose and one purpose only, to get me off. Whether it was literary, auditory, visual, or some combo of all three (as in film), porn was intended to either excite me to the point where I'd seek immediate sex—or, more likely, immediate satisfaction. Once its purpose was achieved, it was put aside, or shut off, or ignored. And once its words and images were no longer fresh and it therefore no longer possessed the ability to excite, it was put away for good, even discarded. Above all, porn was practical, to the point, functional.

Erotica might also get me off. But it seemed to have a second, a third, even more lives: it came to possess a life inside my mind which only the artiest of pornography ever achieved (I think of the mysterious, shadowy, incredibly sexy film *Bijou,* in particular), a continued existence where it began to relate to other books, films, pieces of music, even memories of my own. From speaking to others, I've concluded this might not be peculiar to myself, but is a more generalized effect upon a good-sized proportion of the gay population. Which is why some non-pornographic art—mainstream films (*The Year of Living Dangerously*, say), music (Madonna's "Like a Virgin," perhaps), artwork (Salvador Dali and Caravaggio) and books (James Purdy's *Eustace Chisolm and the Works*) succeed in remaining as particularized touchstones with very strong erotic charges, while others—most famously for me, the novels of Jean Genet—do not.

For others, the Genet novels work brilliantly as fiction and as erotica. For Edmund White, for example, who ended up writing an entire lengthy study/biography of the Frenchman. While what I read when I pick up his fiction is what I suspected Genet actually intended: a piece of masturbation material. Parse any chapter of *Our Lady of the Flowers*, *The Thief's Journal* or *Querelle* and what you have is an endlessly circular writing that builds carefully, detail by detail, action by action (I almost wrote stroke by stroke), up to and then suddenly away again from a climax, only to begin all over again, looping over and over. Isn't that the way most human minds fantasize while masturbating? I can just picture Genet in jail—where he wrote these novels—masturbating as he wrote. Or rather *being unable to masturbate* because he was being watched by other prisoners or guards and therefore using the writing itself as a displaced order of self-gratification. His poetry, also written from a jail cell, is equally incantatory and masturbatory, while his plays—written in freedom—are something different, less looping, more purely narrative.

Some day, read the journals of Casanova's "conquests" or check out Frank Harris' wonderful under-read *My Life and Loves* (with his detailed experiments in gay male lovemaking) and you'll encounter the same rise toward and then suddenly away from a climax, looping again and again.

The Genet discussion raises a kindred point: because we can accept the fact that writing books can be an erotic, even masturbatory act, then what about *reading* books? Isn't reading a book (as opposed to reading bulkier, more physically active newspapers or magazines) in several ways also an erotic act? Perhaps even one of the most erotic of acts we regularly perform?

How do *you* read a book? In a chair, comfortably, feet out on an ottoman? Possibly. Or do you sit sideways, with one or both legs thrown across an arm of the chair? Do you fold your legs up and under you? People do. Or...are you sitting alert, at attention, your feet flat on the ground? Do you perhaps read books in bed, heaps of pillows or a bolster behind you? Or do you prefer a sofa? a lounger? a chaise?...I thought so.

What's nearby as you read a book? A drink? A snack?...yeah, sure. Is music playing in the background? Uh-huh. Are the windows open to a breeze, or is the fan or the air conditioner running on a hot afternoon? Or are the windows locked shut, blinds drawn tightly, the heater chugging, the fireplace ablaze, logs crackling on chilly days?...Um-hmmm. Do you turn off the phone once you settle in, or at least switch on the speaker phone or answer mode, so you don't have to respond?...I guessed as much.

What other sensual acts—in the pure, real meaning of the word, as in using your five senses—are you involved in while you read a book? Touch, of course. The specific dimensions and shape and cover and paper of the book you're holding, to begin with. The cover can range from slickly smooth plasticene paperbacks to ribbed vellum and Morocco leather. Are you sight impaired? Then tactile is the major sense you use reading a book—braille.

Smell? Sure, the smell of a book's paper. Is it new? That smells one way. Crisp. A bit acidic even. Or is it a decade old? That smells another way. Or is it yellowing, crumbling off in flakes. That smells different again. Can you smell the cover material? The glue used to hold it together? Sometimes you can, your face is only inches away from the book.

Many reading addicts add taste to the experience: that nearby drink or dish full of m&m's. Some actually chew the paper or covers. Don't deny it. I've seen you!

Still others add sound—music or the TV is on, turned low, a room or two away. Or the sounds of the outdoors. Or the non-sound of silence, say in a post-midnight reading session, when everyone is asleep and there's only the occasional distant swoosh of a passing auto. I know one woman who reads best outdoors: she likes the birdsong and constant rustling of trees and bushes, the unceasing surf of a beach. I know several fully-sighted people who prefer to listen to books read to them while they're driving. Never a great reader, one friend became a West Coast commuter of two hours per day minimum, and therefore via his car's cassette player, brilliantly well-read. He's way ahead of us on new fiction and non-fiction.

Another pal has to make a nest to read in. I've seen him go through *Entertainment Weekly* standing, wobbling on the subway, seen him peruse *Newsweek* uncomfortably seated waiting in a dentist's anteroom, seen him scan *The New Yorker* on line at his bank. But to feel completely comfy enough to a read a book, he requires a car's entire back seat lined with pillows, a railroad or airplane seat with a pillow placed right here, blanket exactly there, his coat wedged in just so.

The use of the sense of sight in reading books goes without saying, right? It's the sense most of us use the most while reading. But wait. You're using the sense in other ways when you read. When I became a small press publisher several decades ago, publishing up to eight books a year, I also inadvertently became expert in making books, actually producing them. As a result of that experience I can now discriminate among hundreds of shades—between "ante-bellum-vellum" and "palest blue snow"—where you may only see a bunch of white paper. More, I can now discern a medium dark green-black ink from a medium dark blue-black ink, and pick out medium grays from medium-brown grays. I know dozens of text typefaces by sight, the way I know people's faces, and another dozen score of headline typefaces, used for covers, front pages, subtitles. You may not know any. But take it from me, who designed close to a hundred books, they are all part of your unconscious visual experience when reading.

Let me ask that question again: can reading itself be a sensual experience? An erotic experience? What do you think?

Digby J. Lustgarden's Daring Device

Simon Sheppard

Nothing much had been happening, nothing all the way to the flat Kansas horizon. Nothing much had happened since the Gales' house had been swept away by a tornado, and that was three years before. And then one day, up from that big, blank horizon, starting tiny and becoming life-size bit by bit, came a tired old horse slowly pulling a gaudy wagon.

It belonged to a peddler of snake oil, a charlatan on wheels. BROTHER DIGBY J. LUSTGARDEN'S TRAVELING SALVATION SHOW, read the ornate black-and-gold lettering on the wagon's red wooden sides. And then, beneath that, smaller but not much, THE ORGASMATRON, SAVIOR OF MANKIND.

Hardly anyone noticed its arrival. Red-headed Eb Rockett did, out working in the dusty fields, stripped to the waist, sweat pouring down his hard, golden torso. The Kramers, Larsen and Pru, heading the other way down the rutted road, ventured nods from their wagon and received a nod in return. That was about it. But word trickled around, and by late the next morning, Sunday morning, churchgoers in their best clothes had made their way to a field on the edge of town, curious to see what was what. It was maybe a mite sinful of them, it being Sunday and all, but there the tent was, patched and listing a bit, and the crimson-red wagon next to it. And in front of the wagon, standing on a little wood platform, was an exotic young man of exceptional beauty.

"I'm Doctor Lao," he announced when a goodly crowd had gathered. "Spelled L-A-O, pronounced 'Low.' An Oriental name, for I was an orphan, raised by missionaries, and I learned my trade in the Mystic East." So far, the spiel was standard issue; the Kramers, back from wherever they had gone, exchanged knowing glances. *We may be hayseeds*, the glances seemed to say, *but rubes we are not*. But what came next surely piqued the crowd's attention. "My employer Brother Lustgarden and I have come to your town to bring you the blessings of the invention of the millennium, a revolutionary machine of our own devising. The Orgasmatron, my friends, is a miraculous mechanism guaranteed to improve marital relations between newlyweds and the silver-haired alike, and moreover to provide solace for the lonely bachelor." Here, Lao glanced over at Eb Rockett. A significant glance. "And it is possible to do all this with the greatest of ease and comfort, at negligible cost to you. Now then, since the Orgasmatron is to be used solely by the male of the species, we are giving every gentleman in this locale the opportunity to take advantage of its wonders. There will be a meeting this evening, in this very tent, for any man and every man who wishes to attend. Seven o'clock. No cost, no obligation. And now, my friends, I bid you Good Day."

By the evening, nary a man for miles around hadn't heard of the Orgasmatron, and though many were a mite too shy to admit that anything could improve their love life, by seven o'clock the shabby little tent was full to bursting. At the rear of the tent, a large object had been covered by a canvas drape, and from behind the shrouded object appeared Doctor Lao, dressed in a black silk jacket of Oriental design.

"Gentlemen," said the handsome young man, "thank you all for coming. I pledge that you shall not feel your time has been wasted. Here to explain the wonders of the Orgasmatron, miracle machine of the century, is its inventor, Brother Digby J. Lustgarden."

Lustgarden strode out from behind the draped object. The inventor was a man in his mid-forties, of more than moderate attractiveness, with regular features and a tall, well-proportioned body. His trim goatee, flecked with gray, reminded more than one attendee of Beelzebub himself. Lustgarden gave a short talk, explaining the many benefits of his amazing machine, how it could spice up a flagging marriage, cure nagging impotence, and make a lonesome bachelor feel fulfilled. He read testimonial letters from satisfied clients and expounded upon the schedule of fees. Eb Rockett looked around the tent. Many a farmer had a look—not of wonder, but of skepticism and boredom. For even in that corner of Kansas, scalawags with something to sell were anything but rare.

Then, with a flourish, Lustgarden and Lao reached up and whisked the drape from the Orgasmatron. A gasp went up from the crowd. The machine gleamed in the light of the tent's bare electric bulbs.

The elaborate device stood a good ten feet tall, and much of it was painted red, the same devilish hue as the wagon. Brass fittings, bellows and pistons, thick leather straps with silvery buckles—the Orgasmatron was a thing of beauty. A control panel with gauges, switches and small electric bulbs stood to one side of the console. At the other side, a wrought-iron rack held several large dry-cell batteries, ready to lend their power to this miracle of sex. Ornate and beautiful, the Orgasmatron challenged one and all to taste its potent pleasures.

"Who, then," asked Brother Lustgarden, "will be the first of you to experience this miracle of science?"

Not one taciturn Kansan in the audience stirred.

"Gentleman, I know there's some reluctance on your part to surrender hard-earned cash for benefits yet unproven. So what I propose, my friends, is to allow one of you to experience the Orgasmatron first-hand at no cost, risk, or obligation. Which one of you shall it be?"

There still came no response. Then Larsen Kramer stirred. He hadn't intended to; the difficulties that had overtaken his marital relations with Pru had been a well-kept secret. But something in him dared to raise a hand, though when he looked around and met the stares of his friends and neighbors, and felt hot blood rush to his cheeks, Larsen Kramer wished he had kept his hand down, where it belonged.

"Are you sure that's absolutely necessary?" Kramer felt a blush emblazoning his face; though all his neighbors had long gone home, he still felt shy.

"Yes indeed," said Doctor Lao. "A thorough physical exam's a necessity if you're to undergo treatment. Now remove your clothes. All of them."

Kramer stripped to his undershorts.

"What's wrong, Mr. Kramer? Why the hesitation?" Lustgarden prodded. "You have, I assure you, no reason to feel embarrassed." *No matter how tiny it is*, he added silently.

But when the farmer did let his undershorts fall to his ankles, Lao let out an involuntary gasp. Larsen Kramer's penis was one of the biggest, prettiest, most mouthwatering pieces of meat he'd ever laid eyes upon. No, not "one of the biggest." *The* biggest.

"Well, now," said Lustgarden in a slightly mocking voice, "I can certainly see how your wife might have trouble coping with *that*."

Kramer's blush grew even deeper. And, despite his finer instincts, his dick began to swell.

"Listen, this was all a mistake. Maybe I should just get dressed and—"

"Nonsense," said Lustgarden. "Let's just begin…" his hand shot to Kramer's cock "…the examination." He held tight to the big dick, feeling its glowing warmth as it swelled with blood.

"He has good genital reactions, wouldn't you say, doctor?" said Lustgarden, squeezing so hard that the cockhead grew shiny and purple. Kramer felt faint. He looked down at his aching dick. Already, a shiny pearl of precum glistened at the piss-slit.

"The ring?" asked Lao.

"The ring," confirmed Lustgarden. He took a shiny chromium-plated ring from the examining table at his side. While Doctor Lao tugged at Kramer's dick, Lustgarden snapped the hinged ring around the base of the farmer's cock and balls. The shiny metal winked from the bush of wiry brown hair.

Doctor Lao took his hand away. Kramer's dick remained engorged, jutting up from his lean belly, huge.

"A prodigious organ indeed," smiled handsome young Doctor Lao. "Now bend over the examining table."

"What?"

"He said bend over!" Lustgarden snapped. "Are you deaf as well as impotent?"

"Oh, hardly impotent, Digby," Lao smiled, eyes locked on Kramer's huge hard-on.

"With his wife, I mean. Now then, Mr. Kramer," Lustgarden said sternly, "bend over."

Kramer did as he was told. Directly in front of him, a Mason jar of grease sat on the table. He could see Lao dipping his fingers into the jar, then felt Lustgarden spreading the cheeks of his butt, Lao slipping his delicate lubed finger inside him. He started to tense up, to protest.

"Just relax, son," Lao said gently. "Keep breathing and this won't hurt a bit. We just have to make sure that you're a suitable prospect for Orgasmatron therapy."

"And *is* he suitable, Doctor Lao?'

"Suitable indeed, Brother Lustgarden."

And in fact, Lao's expert fingers, probing deep inside Kramer, were sending shivers of pleasure up the farmer's spine.

"Now then, Mr. Kramer, an insertion of the anal probe, and

your pre-treatment examination will be done." Lustgarden held a long chromed-metal tube before Larsen's eyes, an evil-looking tube, about two inches in diameter, tapered at one end, wires leading out of the other. Lustgarden stuck the probe into the grease, then handed it to Lao. The fingers came out of Kramer's ass. The cold, slick tube slid in. The naked man gasped. The click of a flipped switch, and the tube grew warm, began to vibrate.

"Now then," asked Doctor Lao, "how does that feel?"

"It feels," said Larsen Kramer, "really, really good."

By the next afternoon, word had shot round Bradbury Falls, Kansas. Larsen Kramer had, after much electrical humming was heard and a flash or two of light was seen, emerged from Brother Lustgarden's tent with a big old smile on his face. And when his wife Pru appeared in town next morning, she had a big old smile on hers.

"It would be worth whatever its cost," Kramer would say when asked, but would disclose no more than that.

Word of mouth brought several other likely candidates for treatment to Lao and Lustgarden's tent. But it also brought a visitor who, while not unexpected, was nonetheless unwelcome.

The Reverend Micah Pearlbiter, dewlaps aquiver, wasted no time in coming to the point. "It's not merely that you did business on the Sabbath. It's the nature of your business. It's...it's...it's..."

"Unnatural? Perverted? Ungodly?" Lustgarden helpfully offered.

"It's the sort of thing we don't need in a town like Bradbury Falls."

"On the contrary, Reverend," said Lustgarden, all silky-sweet persuasion, "it seems there's a crying need for our services. We have come, not to promote immorality, but to give back to suffering mankind the pleasure which God intended him to enjoy. Just ask Mr. Kramer. Ask his wife."

But Pearlbiter would have none of it. He left an ultimatum in his wake: be out of town by the following morning or face the consequences. "Not here, of course, but in the surrounding towns, there are men who would not hesitate to take matters into their own hands. I cannot be responsible for their actions. This warning, I hope, should be sufficient."

And the Reverend Pearlbiter, lumbering heavily from the tent, gave a single backward glance, full of contempt and dislike, and was gone.

Late in the afternoon, after the treatments of Josiah Dole and Parker Bunn, and after Jim Dalworthy balked at the physical exam and left in a huff, Doctor Lao took a break for business and strolled to Parmalee's General Store for supplies. Just by the feedlot, Lao ran into Eb Rockett. He recalled how Rockett's naked torso, dripping with sweat, straining in the sun, had looked when they'd first approached town.

"Good afternoon," said Lao.

"Afternoon."

"You haven't been by for an exam and possible treatment." Lao's dark eyes flashed significantly. "I would have bet you'd be one of the first."

"Not interested."

"That's blunt."

"Listen, you can fool some of the other men in town, but that machine of yours doesn't do diddly-squat. Guys just think it's doing them some good. But really, they're just fine to begin with. All that folderol just gives them back their belief in themselves."

"Is that so?" Lao slid his eyes from the fieldhand's handsome, craggy face, over his muscular torso, down to his crotch. Noticing, Rockett clasped his hands in front of his basket.

"Yeah, that's so. But I don't need some jumped-up fake doctor to tell me who I am, not at some fancy price. I know who I am and what I want."

"Do tell." Lao moved his gaze back upward, locking his eyes on

Rockett's. His gaze was piercing but his voice was soft. "Well, how about this, my friend? I'd like to offer you the benefits of the Orgasmatron at absolutely no cost to you. Free. Gratis. No obligation. And you can call a halt to the treatment at any time. That's how sure I am that you'll change your mind. Can't be much fairer than that."

"Don't think so."

"Is that a 'no'?" purred Lao.

"Said I don't think so."

"Well, if you should change your mind, you know where we'll be." Lao extended his hand. Eb Rockett had no choice but to unclasp his hands and shake. Rockett's dick was, as Lao knew it would be, noticeably hard.

"Haven't made too much money, Dig."

"Well, what do you expect from a one-horse town like this?" Lustgarden puffed on his pipe. Rings of cherry-scented smoke swirled in the evening air.

"Still, Dig, the sight of Kramer's big fat dick was damn near worth the trip." Lao grinned.

"And then there's that yokel Rockett," said Brother Lustgarden. "It would be fun to get *him* strapped into the old Orgasmatron."

"A bit surly, if you ask me."

"Just the way I like 'em, Lao. Makes breaking 'em down all the more fun."

A voice from outside the tent: "Anybody there?"

"Who's that?" Lao called, but he already knew.

"Eb Rockett."

Brother Digby J. Lustgarden puffed a parade of smoke rings into the Kansas air. "Well," he slyly smiled, "speak of the devil."

"Now then," asked Doctor Lao, "how does that feel?"

"It feels," said Eb Rockett, "really, really good."

"Well, Doctor, it seems that Mr. Rockett here's a suitable candidate for treatment."

"It does indeed, Brother Lustgarden."

Lao slid the warm, pulsing probe out of the naked farm hand's ass. Slowly, Rockett rose from the examining table, his Kansan dick hard, his eyes still half-closed in pleasure.

"Then let the treatment begin," said Lustgarden.

Handsome Doctor Lao walked to the Orgasmatron, which stood almost invisible, draped and unlit in a dim corner of the tent. He pulled the drape aside and threw a switch. The great machine sprang to life, its lights ablaze, its gears and axles humming, its bellows erect with air.

"This way, Mr. Rockett. Step up on that platform." Eb Rockett stepped up onto a shiny metal platform, cold against his bare feet. "Turn around, back to the machine, and spread your legs."

Lao bent down and fastened metal clamps around Rockett's bare feet and ankles.

"Raise your hands above your head."

With broad leather wrist cuffs, Doctor Lao manacled Rockett's hands to the structure of the Orgasmatron. Then he picked up a broad leather band not unlike a small, black corset, drew it around Rockett's waist, and laced it up. Reaching between the naked man's sinewy thighs, he grabbed two straps hanging from the back of the waistband, guided them between Rockett's legs to either side of his hefty ballsac, and through two buckles on the front of the corset-like device. Shiny metal clips hung from the sides of the tightly-cinched waistband; these he fastened two big chromed rings on the Orgasmatron. Surprisingly, Rockett found this constriction of his naked body to be a not altogether unpleasant experience.

Lao stepped back to admire his handiwork. The naked young man's lean, well-muscled form was securely fastened to the machine, his hard, jutting dick shining pink against the tight black corset.

"Perhaps, Brother Lustgarden, you'd like to do the honors?"

"Indeed I would, Doctor Lao."

The older man strode to the great and powerful machine which he'd created. "It's time to hook you up, Mr. Rockett," he said, seizing two electrical cables that sprouted from the Orgasmatron. Lustgarden smiled. "There may be some initial discomfort." There were shiny clamps on the free ends of the cables. He clipped them to Rockett's nipples. The field hand grimaced and writhed, but soon the sensation changed from pain to something approaching pleasure.

Lustgarden clipped two more cables to the ring around the base of Eb Rockett's stiff dick. Then he reached down between Rockett's bare and shackled feet, opened a small door in the platform, and pulled out a gleaming brass fixture, about the size of two large fists, connected to a long tube. He grabbed Rockett's hot, hard dick with one hand and guided the brass fixture over it with the other. The inside of the fixture was as soft and welcoming as the exterior was hard and unyielding; it seemed to gobble up Rockett's flesh, caressing and shaping itself to every curve and contour. Lustgarden fastened down a knurled adjusting knob, then hooked the device to links of chain hanging from the corset.

"And lastly, that sensitive, responsive hole of yours." He reached between Rockett's legs into a compartment, pulled out a larger version of the first anal probe, wires bristling from its base, and guided it home.

Lustgarden stood up and gazed at Eb Rockett. The connecting process always got his dick hard. There was something about having a man, a man like good looking, muscular Eb, spread naked before him, shackled to his machine, connected to his creation, vulnerable, nervous, and not yet understanding the pleasures that awaited him. Digby J. Lustgarden's dick was throbbing.

He looked Rockett in the eye. "I'm about to put a hood over your head, young man. Should you at any time experience discomfort, you have merely to cry out and the treatment will come to an immediate halt. But should you believe that the pleasure you feel is becoming too great, I'd recommend you attempt to relax and enjoy yourself. But, once again, if you *should* cry out..."

And he slipped the black leather hood over Rockett's head.

Standing there connected to the Orgasmatron, the young man's naked body was a work of art. Vulnerable flesh, tan torso, paler legs, coppery hair gleaming in the electric light. The redhead's freckled skin, which sweat had lent a metallic sheen, was restricted, interrupted, and defined by black leather, silvery chrome, and brass. Strapped into the Orgasmatron, Rockett was not so much held captive by the great machine as incorporated into it, its single most vital component.

"You know," said Lustgarden, not particularly kindly, "from the moment we saw you out in the fields, we knew that you'd end up here, strapped into the Orgasmatron."

And then he threw the switch.

The machine came to life, fitfully at first as pistons fired up and bellows filled with air, then settling into a steady, seductive rhythm. Digby J. Lustgarden gazed at his machine, wonderstruck despite his own cynical self, by what he had created. The arcing of blue sparks, the jiggling of needles against calibrated dials. The whirr of gears. The thrusting of pneumatic cylinders, in and out, in and out. The flow of lucent fluids through transparent tubes. And at its center, bound into the clockwork precision of his great life's work, golden against the crimson panels, a vibrant chunk of pulsing, naked human flesh.

Lustgarden looked at Doctor Lao, Lao at Lustgarden. Both their dicks were throbbing hard.

Within the confines of the black cowhide hood, the last of Eb Rockett's qualms had been swept away. As the Orgasmatron had powered up, he'd felt reluctance, uncertainty, yes, even fear. But the first gentle proddings of the machine soothed and reassured, left him receptive for what was to come. A gentle flow of current made his nipples tingle. The velvety touch of the cockpiece stroked his engorged prick. And the probe inside his butt, as it warmed and vibrated, relaxed and soothed his asshole.

The hood left him sightless, but he could still hear the rhythmic sighs and clicks of the machine, pneumatic soughs, flywheels' whirrings. When he opened his mouth to moan in mounting pleasure, a gentle tube snaked from the hood into his mouth, a mechanistic kiss.

The current to his nipples grew more intense, sending jolts of pleasure down his torso to his dick, then down through his throbbing legs to the metal beneath his bare feet. He tried to buck his hips forward, was restrained by the corset. But the dicksheath responded to each thrust, increasing its soft vacuum, enlarging the hard cock.

The machine could read the signs, knew when to increase tempo, what to stroke and when. Rockett's warm body pressed into it. His tongue was against its own. Rockett's cock was filling its receptor, drenching it with precum. His ass welcomed it inside. The Orgasmatron extended the inner piston tentatively from the metal anal probe. Its thrust was answered by a shudder of pleasure. The Orgasmatron retracted the slippery inner cylinder, then thrust it out again, accelerating the pace in sync with the pulsings of Rockett's ass.

The Orgasmatron knew the calibrations of desire. Satisfied with Rockett's responses, it increased the pace, sent more and more sensations surging through the man's flesh. Until it was satisfied.

Together they moved in unison, the machine offering, Rockett receiving, the man thrusting, machine sucking in. As the Orgasmatron accelerated, its humming grew louder, harmonizing with Rockett's groans and sighs. The Orgasmatron held Eb Rockett tight in its embrace, taking him to ecstasies he'd never felt before. His nipples were alive, the sensations in his penis engulfed his whole body, his consciousness was conquered by the feelings inside his ass. He would do anything to please his all-embracing partner, give it everything: his love, his desire, his surrender. The pleasure became so intense, too intense, but he could not, he would not cry out for this to stop. He and this machine would spiral upward, into a tension of lust few had known, into a release that none could understand.

And that release, when it did come at last, brought with it a flash of blinding white light that could be seen for miles around.

The tubes and probes removed, Lao and Lustgarden unbuckled and untied the man, then lifted his sweaty, limp body down from the machine. Weak as a kitten, one arm around each man's shoulders, Eb Rockett looked at these two strangers, then at the huge and gleaming device they'd brought to town, the truth they'd brought into his little life. And he began to sob.

"I understand," said Lustgarden, softly. "You can stay with us here as long as you need to. As long as you like." And so Rockett spent the night, sleeping between the two handsome men, the best night's sleep he'd had in years. Spent the night with all three of them, really—Lustgarden, Lao, and the Orgasmatron.

When Eb Rockett emerged from the tent bright and early the next morning, it did not go unnoticed by others in Bradbury Falls. And this brought a fresh aspect of scandal to the enterprise, though in the weeks to come, whenever Rockett faced whisperings and strange looks, he never gave in, never surrendered his memories of joy and pride and satisfaction. Never apologized, not even to himself.

Still, the new gossip did not help Lustgarden's business. Only a very few men, the brave and the desperate, showed up that day. And when evening fell, the area around the shabby tent was quiet and deserted.

Until a wagonload of men pulled up. And then a second, and a third. Angry men, some dressed in sheets and hoods, many with torches in their hands.

"Come on out, you bastards, so that we can see you," one of them yelled. "We want to see you scum-sucking perverts face to face."

"This is a good Christian town, in a good Christian state, and we don't want you dumb fucks anywhere near our families," another shouted.

"Get out of here," a general chorus rose. "Get out of town and go straight to hell!"

Lustgarden and Lao walked out of the tent and stood side by side, looking frightened but firm.

"Well, looky here," a man in a white sheet cackled. "One of 'em ain't even American."

"I suppose," Lustgarden began, "it's no use trying to reason with you gentlemen…"

"We've heard all we need to know," one red-faced man snapped. "We're gonna tar and feather you, string you up if we feel like it, and burn your den of damnation to the ground."

Several men with torches started walking toward the tent. There was a movement at the tent door. A man emerged. "Why don't you boys all calm down and go home?" said the Reverend Micah Pearlbiter.

"Reverend! What the hell you doin' here?" said a red-faced man.

"Men, friends and neighbors, I once thought as you did, that these men were evil and their machine a device of the devil. But now I have learned differently." A strange look flitted across Pearlbiter's face. "And I am here to tell you that these men are doing the work of the Lord, and their efforts must be allowed to continue unmolested."

There was a stirring in the crowd, mutters of disbelief. "So you, Robertson, and you, Buchanan…." He gestured at a fat man in a hood and sheet. "Go on home and cool down. Let these two good gentlemen get on about their business. Don't make trouble here. Not unless you'd like to deal with my very good friend Sheriff Nielsen."

There was some grumbling, but the fight had gone out of the mob. In a matter of minutes, they'd packed up their torches, gotten back on the wagons, and gone.

Only Lustgarden, Lao, and Pearlbiter were left standing in the moonlight. Without another word, the Reverend smiled at the other two, nodded good-bye, and headed for home. Lustgarden looked at Lao, and Lao at Lustgarden. The moon shone bright.

Next morning, when the sun rose above the flat horizon and the roosters sang out their song, the little patch of ground where the tent had stood was vacant, the men and their machine long gone. They were never to return to Bradbury Falls, though every once in a while there were rumors of their arrival in one Midwestern town or another. The reports sometimes prompted somebody or other to leave town in search of them, with what success one cannot say. But as the months and years went by, these reports grew fewer and finally stopped altogether.

The following Spring, Pru Kramer had the first of what were to be five children. Eb Rockett never married, but he worked hard, saved his money, and was finally able to afford a little farm of his own, and as he grew older, he hired a succession of strapping young men to help him out. Rumors of scandal drove Reverend Pearlbiter far from Bradbury Falls. He headed for a flock in North Dakota, thence to parts unknown.

Brother Digby J. Lustgarden and Doctor Lao are long gone, of course, gone to their final rewards.

But recently, rumors have surfaced that somewhere, in some warehouse out on the plains, the Orgasmatron sits, crated up and waiting patiently to be rediscovered. In this modern age, such a machine seems quaint and obsolete and altogether unnecessary. Of course, we're at ease with our sexuality. There's nothing we don't know about sex. Even if it did exist, no one would admit to being in need of the Orgasmatron.

On second thought, it might be worth the search.

Yellow

Kirk Read

Mama died peaceful. She didn't want us wailing and squeezing her hands as she made her exit, and she knew the only way she'd win was to beat our planes. The neighbors had called us all, seven kids, and said "Come now, 'cause she's close." We'd obliged, hopping into bereavement-discounted aisle seats to accompany her to the next world. But, as usual, Mama got her way.

By the time I got there, she'd been gathered up into a neat pile of bones and taken away for cremation. She wasted no time, even in death. Slow was never Mama's way.

I arrived after midnight. Mama had died that morning, and everyone else was sound asleep or staying at a motel. From the cars out front, I figured that my brothers Dennis and Troy were home, and my Aunt Ruth was in the guest house. She was always in the guest house. Dennis and Troy, no doubt, were passed out in their childhood beds. They drank hard, and they drank for hard sleep. The boys had all left home. My four sisters lived nearby with their families. Mama had always talked about getting us all out of the house so she could have some peace, but none of our childhood rooms had been redecorated.

So I was alone in the house with nothing but the smell of my Mama and the sight of hallways stacked so high with boxes that you could barely pass without elbowing the packed-up remains of one ancestor or another.

I'd known for years I'd be responsible for all this splendor, the scattered belongings of my parents. Mama always told me that as the baby, I was bound to turn out right. I stopped in front of the hallway mirror and looked at myself. I saw the baby Mama had loved hardest. The crushed beer cans in the background confirmed that my brothers were home. They lined the mantle in the living room with the precision only drunks can muster.

Six—no, eight—cans stood proudly under the portrait of my grandfather. Between the third and fourth cans was the urn Mama had rescued from the fire that took up our first house. It had held many Entsmingers, plus one beloved neighbor, and was about to be filled again.

I turned back to the mirror. I was an orphan now—a dazed, blush-stained orphan. I walked into the bathroom and stared into the full-length mirror opposite the sink. I turned the water to hot, stripped off my clothes, and stood, mesmerized by my reflection.

A few days earlier, I'd asked a barber to buzz my reddish brown hair "so I could see skin on the sides." My green eyes, changeable as a mood ring, were muddy, and missed the shield of my unruly bowl cut. I wondered when my cheeks would grow out of their perpetual blush. At that moment, I felt eleven years old. I figured I might as well look it.

I reached onto the counter for what appeared to be the only razor in the house. My brothers, too shiftless to replace or purchase razors, shared until they bled. I lathered my body, armpits to ankles, with the shaving cream Mama had stopped using on her legs six months ago. Slowly, with insistent strokes, I removed every offending trace of adulthood. Hair by hair, I scraped away the years. I was thorough. I knew I'd need to remove every follicle, from the knuckles of my fingers to the swollen joints of my toes.

I ran my fingers over the tiny boy mound of my groin, now cool and hairless. I rubbed circles over the skin and traced a path to the inside of my asscheeks, which were damp and scraped clean. I was again the rosy-cheeked boy who stuffed stolen grocery store candy into the side pockets of Mama's purse.

I opened the cabinet and pulled out one of the diapers we'd put on Daddy when he was getting ready to leave us. Having changed Daddy a thousand times, Mama wouldn't let a diaper touch her hips.

"Just pile towels under me," she said. "That's why God made washing machines."

I pulled the adhesive strips into a tight fit around my waist. I ran my fingertips from the prominent bones in my ribcage down to the place where my hipbones gave way to flesh so tender it tickled when anyone touched it. At 5'6", I was still the runt of the family.

I turned out the light. The plastic sounded like a distant fire as I walked into the hallway. I reached into the blackness and pulled down the steps to the attic.

I'd been up there so many times I trusted the dark. I felt my way through instinct and memory to the dim corner under the skylight. Hanging on a piece of fish line was the mobile I'd had over my crib. I turned on the bulb. Amazingly, it still worked, and dozens of yellow pinpoints of light filled the attic. It's a wonder every child in my family wasn't epileptic.

Beneath the mobile stood our family crib, the post-womb home for all of Mama's brood. I'd spent several years climbing out of it, and now I was climbing back in. I was a late walker and talker. Mama always used to point to the places on the crib where I'd gnawed on the wood, saying "You always did like that crib. It kept the boys from throwing you around."

I lay on my back, mesmerized by the lights. The oak crib was huge, more like a puppy cage, with one hinged side that could be lowered to the floor.

I cry until Dennis gets there. Sometimes, when he passes out, the only thing that works is dragging my silver rattle along the side of the crib, like an inmate in some deep county jail. He reaches into the crib, cupping the back of my two-year-old head, holding my skull with his hand, callused at sixteen by chopping firewood. His sandy knuckles rub at the blond wisps on my skull. He hoists me to eye level and pulls me to his chest. I pull the hair sprouting on his chest and bite his collar with the beginnings of teeth. He feeds me two of his fingers. No matter how hard I bite, he never flinches or jerks them away. He stares placidly into my face and rubs his fingertips across my gums. That's when I stop crying.

I reached into the corner for that silver rattle, found it at my feet, and raked it along the slatted sides of the crib. I started on the right, then dragged it over every standing piece of wood, until I was in a frenzy. Soon I was shifting the rattle from hand to hand and hammering the metal into the corners. My brothers always said I was "strong as hell for such a little mutt." I figure it was either from fighting my brothers off or demanding that they pay attention to me. I knew that if Dennis was still breathing, somewhere in this house, he'd be joining me tonight under the yellow lights. I mumbled his name, whispered it, gurgled it up to a scream, until suddenly the rattle flew from my hand. It hit the floor, bounced down the steps to the bedroom-lined hallway below.

I heard footsteps, then the muffled sound of a beer can being crushed. With each creak of the attic steps, I tensed, my skin slick with sweat; I shivered so violently I was almost paralyzed. When I saw the top of his dirty blond head rise over the steps, my skin flooded with goosebumps. I soaked my diaper. My screaming turned into a soft whimper, and a warm sheet of urine trickled over my quivering buns.

Dennis stood over the crib, a cigarette in his right hand, the crushed can in his left. He dropped the can and kicked it into the darkness of the attic. I'd always been able to smell Dennis before I saw him. Mama always said he smelled like a billy goat, but I swapped our pillowcases to smell him until I was eleven, when he moved out for good.

He dropped the expired Winston to the floor, twisted the ball of his bare foot to crush it, and unlatched the hinged side of the crib. He reached down with both hands and gripped my hips, pulling me to him. My butt slid along the sweaty vinyl that lined my childhood bed. My ass was now balanced on the edge of the cushion, my ankles resting in the grooves of the flattened, hinged door.

Neither of us said a word. Two long fingers brushed my cheek, stroked my lips, and wormed gently into my mouth. I closed my lips around his tightly bent fingers and tasted nicotine and gasoline. His other hand reached for my hair, which he was used to tugging. Instead, he rubbed my head like a dog he was about to reward with a biscuit. He fixed his foggy green eyes on my face and matching eyes. Then he winked at me as he undid the snaps of his overalls. They slid to the floor; he stood naked and half hard. I sucked a third finger into my mouth and traced his fingernails, bitten to the quick, with my tongue.

Dennis brushed the palm of his hand from the top of my chest down to the top of my diaper, then sank to his knees to lick my belly. He knew, from years of tormenting me, where I was ticklish, and dragged his tongue, carpet-like from cigarettes, over the skin barely beneath my bellybutton. I bucked, giggled, and kicked. I slapped the side of his head hard enough to make him look up and grin.

He stopped.

He pulled his fingers from my mouth, replaced them with his tongue, heavy with beer and smoke. He cradled my head now with both hands and pulled me to a sitting position. His knuckles, more callused than the last time he held me, moved to my shoulders, then to my hips. He tugged gently at the diaper's adhesive bonds. The jagged skin of his palms brushed against the head of my dick, now poking out the top of the diaper. He pulled down the front and laid it flat against the bedding. His mouth moved over my cock, still warm with piss. He licked me clean, tracing his tongue up over my silky belly, then back down to my cock and around my ballsac, which was bunched up from the chill of the shave. He stretched his lips over his teeth and pulled on my balls. He sucked them so far from my body I thought he was going to swallow them.

I took a deep breath and he let go, wrapping his hand around my sac, which was now stretched thin. He licked precum from my dickhead, catching a few stray drops which had rolled into my belly button. He took my cock deeply into his mouth, his nose rubbing against my pubic bone.

His fingers, still wet with my spit, pushed at my hole. I moaned softly, then felt his middle finger sinking into me. After years of yelling at him for biting his nails, I was now relieved by his habit. He dropped a long stream of spit and worked in his second finger.

With the other hand on the back of my head, Dennis pulled my face to his now throbbing cock. I'd always dreamed about what it would look like hard. As he stood there, hands on his belly, his cock pointed due north. It was so hard it twitched every few seconds. Like mine.

I closed my eyes, opened my mouth, and saw blotches of yellow light through my eyelids. Dennis filled my mouth, shoved so far into my throat that his balls pushed against the tiny cleft in my chin. The two fingers in my ass became three as he again dribbled spit onto my crack, then smeared it over my sphincter.

He was cut, like the rest of us, with the impossibly long, skinny dick God sometimes gives tall boys. He dragged his fingers across my head as his cock picked up speed in my mouth and his fingers plunged deeper into my ass. His cockhead curved gracefully down my throat, then withdrew to the edge of my gums. I was trying like hell to keep up with his thrusts. Drool was running out of the sides of my mouth, and with each thrust, I gripped the sheet beneath us.

Dennis sensed my mouth was tiring, my jaws were numb, and

sank his cock into my throat in one long, slow push. His hand still behind my head, he pulled out and lowered me to the floor. He placed my ankles over the top of the crib, so that I lay back staring into the torrent of spinning yellow light.

Dennis cupped his hand over my mouth, and I filled his palm with spit. He coated his cock with it. He leaned back on the balls of his feet and pulled his fingers from my ass. The sudden void made me shiver. With my propped feet, I lifted my ass from the diaper. Dennis clamped his hands around my hips and worked himself in.

Several handsfull of spit later, we were belly to belly, his cock deep into my hole, and I ached for the relief of an upstroke.

My eyes rolled back. I was mumbling gibberish, the long forgotten language of my infancy. Dennis tightened his grip on my hips, pulling my ass into the air to match his rhythm. Each stroke was heaven until that last excruciating inch. After fifteen minutes of steady pounding, that last inch wasn't any easier. Finally, I bit my tongue. I tasted bittersweet blood on the roof of my mouth.

I clutched the sides of the crib with both hands to steady myself: Dennis had forgotten all about tenderness now and was slamming my ass with the fervor of a careless schoolboy. I took shallow breaths and squeezed my ass muscles as hard as I could around his cock. He gritted his teeth, closed his eyes, and growled like I'd bitten him. His body shook and in wild, angry bursts, he filled my ass. I couldn't tell when he stopped coming, because his pelvis kept slamming into me in wild, involuntary bursts.

He knelt in front of me for what seemed forever, then pulled out slowly, as if removing a Band-Aid. He stood just as slowly, and without saying a word pulled up his overalls, snapped them on, and knelt down again. His cum was dribbling out of my ass, onto the diaper.

Dennis tugged the front of the soaked diaper to my belly, wrapped the wings around my hips, and resealed the adhesive. He covered me with a blanket draped over the side of the crib. He let the blanket waft down over my body as if I were asleep and he didn't want to wake me. He lifted the crib's open side and closed its latch.

He bent down, ran his fingers across my close-shorn scalp, and pressed his lips to my forehead. He retreated to his bedroom. My breathing slowed and deepened, and the spinning yellow lights lulled me to sleep.

Privacy, Please!!!

Michael Lassell

"Lawrence," I said into the cordless, "I am looking at him right now!"

"What's he wearing?" Lawrence asked, cutting as usual to the chase without so much as a hem or a haw. The young are so refreshingly direct.

"Nothing, of course. That's what he's always wearing. If he's home, he's naked. It's the best thing about him."

"Well, if your bedroom has to face an air shaft, it's nice that the landlord provides visual aids."

"It's not an air shaft," I said, truly offended. "It's an interior courtyard with street access, and he doesn't actually live in this building. And my landlord does not supply humpy eye candy. My landlord supplies cockroaches and the occasional rodent we all hope is a large mouse."

Lawrence said something into his cordless that sounded like "I have to take a bowel movement," so it was probably "Why don't you move," because if Lawrence did indeed need to move his bowels, he would be unlikely to say so, thanks to WASP potty training and Ivy League schooling—and if he was going to mention it at all, he most certainly would have said, "I have to take a shit." Anyway, whatever it was, I couldn't hear it because there was a hideous explosion at his end of the line.

"What the fuck was that?" I asked, wondering if I should be alarmed.

"Oh, nothing," Lawrence said wearily. "They're shooting another movie in the vacant lot behind my apartment. Apparently it's an action movie and they're using explosives instead of a script."

"It's one o'clock in the morning," I noted.

"I know, I know. It's been going on for three nights."

"Who's in it?"

"I don't know. Some over-the-hill heterosexual. Chuck van Schwarzenwillis or something."

"Mel Gibson?" I asked.

"He's the homophobic one who used to be cute, right?"

"Right."

"No, it's not him. It's somebody even older than that, and the girl is about thirty seconds past early puberty. I think Hollywood should be arrested for child pornography."

"I didn't realize you had limits with respect to pornography," I said.

"Well," Lawrence answered with a trace of *hauteur* in his well-modulated contralto voice, "I do: I hate action movies."

"Well, come over here, then, and I'll show you an action movie you'll like. It's triple-X rated and stars my very own new neighbor, and it is truly up front and personal."

"What's he doing?" Lawrence asked.

"Working out," I replied, but I was drowned out by the Con Ed crew digging to China at the street-access moment of my alley—er, interior courtyard. Which they had been doing for over a year that I knew about.

"What?" asked Lawrence.

"Working out," I shouted, but the cordless started squawking—

his or mine, who knows?—and we hung up. We were used to it. No matter how many frequencies there are on the airwaves, there are at least ten people in any New York neighborhood with the same one, and they're all on the phone.

My new neighbor was what I would have to call hot. Steamy. Sizzlin'. A livin' doll. He was tall, dark, and drop-dead gorgeous. Latino or Italian was clear to my ethnic ID antenna—although some might have guessed Greek, and had he been a little less bulky, one might even be forgiven for thinking him Persian. But he was bulky. Gym-bunny bulky. His shoulders swelled out about six inches on each side past his actual skeleton, and one of them sported a goofy *Keep on Truckin'* tattoo just like Tony Danza used to have (or maybe still does). This made me think he had probably lived in San Francisco, since he was way too young to have lived through the '70s, and San Francisco is the one city on earth where the '70s have never died. San Francisco plus Latino, of course, meant Mexican.

He had ski-jump pecs capped by a pair of redwood-dark nipples you could use for shelter in a storm. His knotted torso made him look like he was wearing that leather armor they always have on in those Roman bible epics in the '50s (an effect heightened by his skin color, which was some unique tint comprised of caramel, camel, coffee, coconut shell, tropical sunlight about an hour before dusk, and rare gilt-edged volumes of the sixteenth century). Unsurprisingly, he had the legs of a seasoned soccer player. Which meant, of course, that he had one of those asses so beautifully defined and perfectly rounded that it was actually two loaflike masses of fuck-me flesh.

His chest was relatively hairless, which is a turn-on for me if it's natural and a total barfer if it's not. He had a patch of dark hair on his chest nestled between his tits like a little goatee that had fallen off an idolatrous trick, and it kind of trickled over the bricks of his abs, split around his deeply sunken navel like a brook around a boulder, and came to a slightly curlicued tail, so to speak, about one kiss north of his abundant, jet-black pubic hair. He shaved his legs from the knees down, and he did it in his bedroom—not in the shower—which is how I knew, because when he was in the shower, I could only see him from the solar-plexus up.

And did I mention that he had a dick?

It's not that it was so huge, although it was definitely more dinner kielbasa than breakfast link. Or perhaps chorizo is more appropriate to the object at hand (so to speak). It was classic in shape, if you like cut sausage, and I do—maybe because I have one of my own, but also because they're less work (which is why I like summer more than winter: all those layers of clothing getting tangled up with each other every time you enter or exit a room). Which meant, I quickly clocked, that wherever his parents were from, he was probably born (a) in a hospital and (b) in the US of A, a country as irrationally infatuated with circumcision as it is with psychiatry, which may, of course, be related.

Everyone's idea of a perfect dick, is, of course, different. His was mine. Long enough to dangle and sway when he walked, but not enough to scuff his knees, and rather thick, with a slight (and I mean slight) taper before flaring into a rather more-pointed-than-not glans. Erect, it points almost straight up along his torso as if following the path mapped out by the hair that grows along his axis of symmetry. There's an appealing curve to it that suggests the outside arc of rhinoceros horn.

Didn't I mention that I'd seen his dick in copulatory action?

Oh, yes. My new neighbor, who is probably in his mid-to-late twenties, has no shame. He not only walks around naked, but he frequently walks around hard, his usually loose-hanging balls tucking up below that divinely bouncing divining rod. And he's not always alone. I've seen a United Nations of calendar boys pass through that bedroom. I've seen his dick buried to the mustache in the greedy mouths of admiring lads. I've seen him service a procession of well-lubed assholes, pushing in until his pubes start to gleam like the raven tresses of an Andalucian starlet finding her key light, then pulling out again so the puckered scarlet tip of it cleared the welcoming butthole and then jamming back in again.

And I have seen dicks of all description, some of them larger than life, pounding his own glory hallelujah, him screaming in English and Spanish and that language of animal sounds spoken only by men in the climax moments of butt-fucking ecstasy. I've seen him knees-over-head with a family-sized dildo up his butt, and watched him wedge all his fingers into his asshole, not to mention carrots, cucumbers, zucchinis, and even a phallic lube pot. He is as erotically adroit as linguistically versatile.

Apparently he didn't realize that turning off the lights would have made it more difficult to watch him. He also did not seem to understand the principle of shades, blinds, or blackout curtains. And he certainly didn't know every spasm was being appreciated and sometimes—often—accompanied just ten or twelve feet away across an air shaft, by an admiring neighbor who, okay, I admit it—sometimes related the whole scene while it was happening to friends on the phone who were also jerking off just hearing how hot the whole fucking business was.

Or maybe he knew just what he was doing.

"That was so fucking hot," Lawrence said once when we were done.

"I shot over my head," I said into my cordless.

"No shit," he said. "I'd like to see that some time."

"Well, you can't see it unless you get naked over here," I said, following a flirtatious road that had so far led nowhere.

"What's happening with José?" Lawrence asked, for that is what we called him.

"Well the black guy's head is kind of below the window sill at the moment, so I can't really tell if he's lapping up the cum, but that certainly is what I'm guessing from the movements of those dreadlocks."

"Maybe I should come over," Lawrence said.

"I don't think so," I said, since it seemed that José was shifting himself into "Fuck me *now!*" position, a lovely profile view in doggy style that allowed me an excellent vantage point for round two. "I'm going to have to come again, and I don't think I can wait for you."

"I'm definitely coming over tomorrow night," Lawrence said.

"He doesn't do it *every* night," I said.

"I'll take my chance," Lawrence said, and a huge explosion went off on his end of the line.

"Are they still making that fucking movie?" I asked.

"No—I mean, yeah, they are, but I think that was a bomb," Lawrence answered.

Having both hands free was, of course, an advantage because I could work my dick and at least one nipple at the same time. I was on my knees in the dark watching José get hosed when it happened.

I was staring at him taking his "date's" dick up his ass, when José looked straight across the gaping gulf between our buildings and right into my eyes. And then...he winked. Winked! I swear. I blinked my eyes, as if this could not possibly be the case, as if there were no way he could be watching me while I was watching him. But, as if reading my confusion, he picked one hand off the mattress and waved. God knows what else he would have done if his top-of-the-moment hadn't pulled his head around for a near kiss.

Now, New York is a funny place. There are way too many people living in way too small a place, and we've developed a kind of privacy by agreement. We have no privacy so we agree to pretend we have it. Of course we all walk around in underwear or less, but we never, ever "notice" each other through our windows. We would rather be guillotined than mention to a neighbor, whom we've routinely seen muff diving, that she has a nice butt when we see her walking her bulldog.

Watching José get hard while he curled his barbells naked in the window, watching him jerk off after toweling the sweat from his bushy underarms, watching him suck and fuck and get sucked and fucked was all sexier than shit. But none of it was shocking. The wink and the wave were unprecedented. How could I go on living here if people actually acknowledged that we were all watching each other all the time?

Now, I am a quantity shooter, and a distance shooter, too—although my second and third fusillades are usually paltry compared to the first. But something opened up in me when he winked. I crawled across my bed, closer to the window. I was yanking like a madman when the black guy who was fucking José let out a roar that José joined with a scream and that I turned into a trio with a guttural groan loud enough to make my ribs resonate, and I shot straight through the open window and past the fire escape.

José turned and looked. I wondered if I'd hit his window with my cum, but that would have been unlikely for a second shot. I vowed to see if I could make it, though—sometime. Maybe if I stood on the fire escape…

"Hi," José said from behind me in the Korean deli at the corner. I was trying to choose three perfect Bosc pears from the rotting pile on the fruit stand: big, hard, sweet, unbruised.

I was taken, as they say, totally aback.

"Oh, hi," I said.

"I'm José," he said.

"I know," I said.

"You know my work?" he asked.

"Oh…," I said, "…your name is José, I mean, it's really José."

He looked at me as if I were acting strangely.

"Yeah," he said. "It's not that unusual a name."

"Oh, nonono," I said, trying to cover. "It's a great name. Spanish."

"Right," he said. "José Esteban."

I didn't know what to say, so I said nothing, my usual mistake when my dick begins to tingle itself awake in its auburn nest.

Some ancient lesson of civilization came bubbling out of my genes to my conscious mind and I stuck out my hand and said my name.

"I thought maybe you recognized me," he said, oddly earnest.

"Oh," I said, "I do."

"No, no, not from the window," he smiled unselfconsciously, as if that were a forgone conclusion. "From my movies."

"You're an actor?" I asked.

I mean, really, when I'm around a man I want to fuck I might as well be a tourist from Oklahoma who has never seen a city in his life. My blasé native New York attitude goes gurgling down the nearest sewer drain, and I become a shuffle-footed teenager with acne and unsupportive parents. Oh, right—that *was* me.

"No," he said. "I do porn."

"Ohhhhhhh," I said. And I meant it.

"Yeah, you've probably seen me."

"Right. Well, actually, um, no…sorry. I don't actually watch it. I mean, I've seen it, of course—" Christ, now I was insulting his profession.

"It's okay," he said. "It's not for everyone."

"No, no. It's me," I said, although I have no idea what I meant by that.

So of course then there was the first awful empty silence. My years on the streets of Manhattan have at least taught me this fact of life: get past the first awkward silence, and anything is possible; lose the moment, and you'll never get it back.

"Well," he said…

"No, don't go," I said…"um, I mean, unless you have to."

"No. I'm on my way home. I just saw you looking at the fruit…"

"Right," I said. "I'm a big fan of fruit."

He grinned, which kicked off the second horrible empty pause, because I was now mesmerized by him. Happily, the second embarrassing pause is never as bad as the first (you already have empirical evidence that you can survive silence).

"So that explains it," I managed, just because I was wondering if he could tell I couldn't keep my eyes off his nipples, which were bulging through a bright-red, skin-tight T-shirt.

"Explains what?" he said, jumping on his cue.

"Why you're so, um, uninhibited."

"I'm not all that uninhibited," he said, almost shyly, "except sexually."

"Right," I said.

"I like it when you watch me," he said, looking directly into my eyes with eyes that I had not quite noticed before, or at least appreciated. They were the kind of blue that seems to exist only in children's books, not in nature: bright, light, liquid, sharp, intelligent, wild, incongruously northern in his Mediterranean face, but warm as a hearthstone. The kind of aquamarine or turquoise associated with swimming pools and parakeet feathers.

"You knew I was watching?" I said.

"Yeah," he said.

My mind was racing faster than slot machine wheels before they settle on bells, bars, or cherries. I was desperately trying to think of something to say.

"Don't think so hard," he laughed. "I think you're hot."

"You think I'm hot?" I said, or asked, or whatever.

"Absolutely," he replied. "Way. You wanna come up?"

I put my pears back on the pile.

"He's really sweet, Lawrence," I said.

"You slept with him?" Lawrence said for the fourth or fifth time, the amazement in his voice growing with each repetition.

"Yes," I said. "Is that so odd?"

"Oh, no," he lied. "You sleep with dog food all the time," which was our term for those overly beefy Chelsea boys who all want more than anything to look like a meat meal. We have also been known to call them frozen dinners.

"Eat me," I said.

"Was it hot?"

"He's Chicano," I said, not by way of explanation, but to change the subject. "His father was, is, Mexican," I continued. "His mother is half Mexican, half French—which is where the blue eyes come from, or at least that's what he says. He was born in Stockton, went to Diablo Valley Junior College and San Francisco State, has six brothers and sisters, including a lesbian, he's a few credits short of a degree in something business-y, and he's very, very sweet."

"And?" said Lawrence, who knows me better than anyone.

"And he's a porn star."

There was a silence even the bomb going off in the parking lot next to Lawrence's apartment couldn't drown out.

I started counting off the seconds, waiting for Lawrence's response, but I hadn't started right at the beginning, so I gave up counting and broke the silence for him.

"Well, not a star, exactly, which is a word used way too often. I mean, everybody who's ever been in a film calls themselves a star, a superstar, even, but he's on the way up. And he's very—"

"Sweet?"

"Well, yes, he is very sweet."

"And how was the, you know, sex?" Lawrence asked, his voice rising at the end while drawing out the x-sound of sex rather longer than I would have thought humanly possible.

"Well, oddly enough," I said, because that's the kind of relationship we have, "he likes getting fucked the best, which is not what I would guess if I just saw him walking down the street, which, of course, is my favorite thing in the whole world to do. Sexually."

"Maybe I should come over there," Lawrence said.

"Well, it was very nice...you know, sweet and all. He's

almost shy. I liked touching him. He has the stupidest tattoo that ever came out of a needle. He was a big stoner in San Francisco, although he says he's actually in AA now and totally clean and sober, and he got the tattoo one night when he was loaded over in North Beach somewhere. Actually," I continued, "I liked the kissing more than the fucking."

After I put back the pears, I undressed him, of course. I love undressing men.

We walked through the door. He clicked a lock or two behind him, and went to pull off his T-shirt.

"Uh-uh," I said, "let me."

He dropped his arms and looked at me, eye to eye again. My dick was inching up the inside of my Jockeys. He smiled, sweetly. His gave his head a coltish toss to clear his unfashionably long hair out of his eyes.

I put one hand on each side of his waist and moved in so close I could feel the heat from his nostrils on my face. He was maybe an inch shorter than me, so he was a bit under six feet. I ran my hands up the side of his T-shirt, along the seams.

He breathed deeply, exhaling into my face.

I raised one hand and touched his lips with one finger. They were full and fleshy and parted slightly. I moved my lips as close as I could to his without touching. We were both breathing harder. I grabbed his T-shirt in two hands and pulled it roughly up and over his head. Before he brought his arms back down, I put my hands back on him, rubbing his dark-haired underarms with my thumbs, while my fingers put some pressure on his shoulder blades.

I pulled him in closer and his face moved toward mine. Before our lips touched, I blew slightly over them and he opened his a bit more and licked them with the tip of his tongue. I ran the tip of my tongue as gently as I could on the underside of his upper lip, then moved my fingers down to his nipples.

He emitted a loud *whew* and gasped on the inhale when I pinched slightly on each one. I flicked each with the back of my thumbnail and blew a trail of breath down his body until I was kneeling in front of him, breathing through the denim of his Levi's into his bulging basket.

"Put one of your feet here," I said, touching my chest.

He did.

I untied the laces of his boot, slowly, and then pulled it off. Then the sock. His toes were long and straight.

"The other one," I said.

When he was barefoot, I stood up again and put my fingers lightly on each side of his face, barely touching the beard stubble there. I pulled his face forward again and when his lips and mine touched, I dropped one hand to his crotch and barely touched his dick, which was already hard. I opened his belt and the top button, slid down the zipper, peeled back the fabric and let it slip over his hips.

The pants dropped to the floor and he stepped out of them. His dick sprung to flagpole position and he shuddered. He was covered in goose flesh. I slipped one hand behind him, to his upper thigh, and stroked the front of his body with the other. When I got near his crotch, I slipped past his dick and drew my fingertips under his tightening balls. Then I grabbed his balls and pushed my mouth onto his mouth at the same time.

Now, not everyone knows how to kiss. And not every mouth is made for contact. José was born oral. His hot, wet lips nearly melted away and we went at each other's mouths until all the flesh was indistinguishable and we seemed more like kiss than kissing.

The kissing got him going and he started pulling at my clothes. I helped him all I could, because I could not think of anything I wanted to be more than naked and inside him.

As soon as I was as naked as he was, he dropped to his knees and took my cock into his mouth up to the hilt. God bless the gay man's gag-free throat, I thought as I started to rock my hips into a righteous face fuck. He was working me up so fast that I had to pull away before I shot in his mouth. No way I was leaving here without my dick up his ass, and I wanted that particular ejaculation first.

He was totally amenable as I maneuvered him onto his back. He reached across his bed to the windowsill without looking and got a condom in his hand, opened it with his teeth in a single gesture, and started working it onto my dick. I worked his ass with my fingers for a while before slipping my dick into him. I pumped hard and fast, but not long. He was pulling on his own dick with a two-handed grip I'd only seen once before. I wondered if he knew my friend Rob.

"I'm gonna—" he said, and he started to shoot before he was even finished speaking. I pulled out of him and the rubber nearly simultaneously and shot my first beautiful load of the day onto his face and shoulder and the wall behind him and onto the foothills of his mountainous midriff.

"Oh...My...God...!" he shouted. "You fucking shoot!"

It was the least I could do.

When I came out of the shower, José was sitting on his bed, naked of course. Behind him was his bedroom window and fire escape and the air shaft and my fire escape and my window and my bed, which was perfectly visible from here. The desk on the side of the room opposite the bed was even visible. I wondered if he could read what I was writing from here as well as I could read his body from there.

He had one leg crossed over the other, one foot almost in his lap, which reminded me of the lotus position, and he was leaning against the headboard.

"I'm sorry," he said.

"What for?" I asked.

"I wasn't very good," he said.

"You were fabulous," I said, but the truth is, I was disappointed, and wondered if he was picking up on the unspoken. It had been much hotter in my mind than it was in fact, despite the obvious pleasure every cell in my body had taken in the encounter: I was as depleted after a single ejaculation as I've ever been. It was like numbers two and three had pushed up their schedule to rendezvous with the early bird for a serious worm hunt.

"Something was missing," he said, rolling his head toward his window, toward my window, then quickly back. "I know sex, and I know we've got more in us."

"You have sex a lot," I said, sitting next to him on the bed.

"Do I?" he asked. "What's a lot?"

"Well, most days and sometimes more than once a day, sometimes with more than one partner."

"Well, it won't last forever," he said. "I know that. I think it's my duty to my body to use it for sex when it's still in great sexual shape, you know? I mean, it's not the only thing I do. And I'll do other things later when people stop wanting my body. I'll develop my mind. I'll join a monastery or study Buddhism."

He dropped his head to his chest like a little boy who has done something wrong.

"You're really good at sex," I said. "Really open. Undefended. It's unusual. It's...wonderful."

"I hope we can do it again," he said.

"Can and will," I said. "I want to." It was no lie.

"So what was wrong with it?" Lawrence was asking.

"Well, nothing was wrong with it," I was answering. "I mean, it was better than most of the sex I've had in my life. And he is absolutely the most beautiful man I've ever fucked—ever. But it did not rise to my expectations."

"But he wants to get together again."

"Oh, yeah. We actually went out for coffee after and had a long talk. He's not stupid. He's got a lot of ambitions for his life and career. He wants to get out of the sex business after he makes a bundle from his booty. He's actually a great conversationalist. I mean, he doesn't wax eloquent about the Jacobean Shakespeare, but he doesn't go on and on about himself, either. He's informed, interested. And there is definitely more there than meets the eye, even though what meets the eye is more than enough."

"The first time is never the best," Lawrence said with his ordinary extraordinary insight and the kind of intelligence even the Ivy League couldn't ruin.

"He's dancing at the Gaiety this week," I said.

"Yeeww," Lawrence responded acidly, seeming to forget once again that he was nonjudgmental in all things sexual. "Is he fucking the clients behind the movie screen, too?" he asked.

"Lawrence," I said, with mock impatience, "you can't actually have sex with the dancers at the Gaiety any more. You have to take them to a hotel."

"Oh," said Lawrence, with that plaintive note in his voice that signals his conviction he was born too late for all the fun stuff. "Are you going?"

"He wants me to."

"Well, then go."

"Oh, I don't know. I've sort of given up the Gaiety. It just seems depressing and desperate lately."

"Since you can't have sex with the dancers on the premises. You know you're no good at postponed gratification."

Did I mention I had a huge crush on Lawrence when we met and ruined any chance for us making a go of life together by pushing too hard when he said he was ambivalent?

"Thanks for sharing," I said, "but I already have one therapist, *comprende*?"

He *comprende*'d.

"But it was fun back there behind the movie screen," I continued, "getting it on with some fantasy stud while a bunch of other couples were doing the same thing all around you, and the dancers were kind of working up their hard-ons and strutting around naked. And all for forty bucks. Now it's just…I don't know…it's like shopping for lettuce. You go in, they dance around naked, you pick one, you make a deal, you go to a hotel, they do less than you want for the money, they do more than they want to for their heterosexual self-image. Yaddah yaddah yaddah. I don't know. Maybe."

Even these days, as the millennium approaches, the Gaiety Burlesk is a zoo on Friday and Saturday night, when they've got a dozen or more dancers carrying on all night long. The place is packed, humid with lust and cash, and you have to assert yourself to get what you want.

Tuesday afternoon, on the other hand—and just for an example—is an altogether different story. There are six dancers usually. They dance. There's a scene from a porn movie. Another dancer comes out. In between they sit in the smoking lounge hoping to snag a john from the five or six geriatric tourists in the place. But I was off on Tuesday afternoon that week, so that's when I climbed the stairs under the new canvas awning on Forty-Sixth Street. *Titanic* was playing at the theater next door. The phrase "going down" kept repeating itself in my mind. And the word "disaster."

I paid my money to a young man sitting in a booth behind glass and entered a familiar dark world full of rock music.

There was a very well put together Asian dancer on the runway, gyrating his hips and pointing his hard-on off the stage and into the house. I counted four men in the audience. There is a no-sex policy here, thanks to an asshole named Rudy Giuliani, who managed to get himself elected mayor of New York—twice—but at least two of the old geezers were jerking off, which was kind of comforting.

I went into the lounge. A couple of men were sitting there smoking, watching one of the dancers at the ancient video game by the stage door, on which a prominent sign hung that said: PRIVATE. NO PATRONS PAST THIS POINT.

The door swung open, and José appeared, wearing sweat pants, hightops, and a sweatshirt with the sleeves ripped off. It was love at first sight all over again.

"Hi," he said, and gave me a kiss.

The two smoking elders started drooling.

"Come on," he said and led me to the forbidden door.

"You won't get in trouble, will you?" I asked.

"Nah, the old dykes aren't here today," he replied, meaning the gypsy sisters who ran the place and usually presided over the ticket booth like gorgons guarding the Golden Fleece.

Backstage was pretty much the way I remembered it. There was a bleached-blond sitting on a bench in the little locker room trying to get it up with baby oil and a man-woman fuck rag.

José took my hand and walked up a couple of steps. We crossed behind the screen and down the steps on the other side. When we were alone in the little back area where I had shelled out the requisite tariff more than once, he turned to me, lifted his sweatshirt over his head, dropped his sweat pants and pushed his perfect naked body up against me. He started to get hard immediately, his stiffening dick working its way between my legs.

He planted a huge kiss on my mouth but pulled off suddenly.

"Shit," he said. "That's my music. I have to go on. Go out front and watch me," he said. "Sit right in front of the runway. I'll meet you out there when I'm done."

The blond grunted at me huffily as I left. I guessed he was about thirty. He looked fifty.

By the time I got to my appointed (and thankfully uncontested) seat at the foot of the runway, José was already on stage with his shirt and sneakers off.

I sat down and he proceeded to gyrate rhythmically, dancing only for me, stroking his dick through his sweat pants, then pulling open the waist and putting his hands inside.

He twirled around and showed his butt to his audience of one, slipping the pants down off his ass cheeks and flexing his gorgeous gluteus maximus muscles. He bent over far enough, spreading the cheeks with his splayed fingers, to give me an unobstructed, spotlighted view of his happily hospitable hidey-hole in its nest of sweat-sleek hair.

Then he stripped the sweat pants off and turned around. He'd already worked himself into a beautiful boner and dropped himself to his knees at the end of the runway, pulling on his dick and pumping his hips directly at my face. He was smiling and licking his lips and giving me the hypnotic limpid eye all at the same time, while sweat started dripping out his pores and down over the muscles of his belly.

I was as hard in my jeans as I ever get in my jeans, and I was rubbing my sweaty palms on my thighs when the music ended and the lights went down to the sound of two or three entranced old-timers applauding limply.

I was still sitting there when the movie started up again and José came into the house wiping the sweat off his trunk with his sweatshirt. He was ignoring the man trailing him and gave me a gesture to follow him.

"Sit with me a while," he said, and led me to the back row of the theater, where three seats sat in virtual darkness between the projection booth on one side and the corridor wall on the other.

We sat down. I put my arm around the back of his chair and he put his hand on my thigh. I was still hard, which he found out almost instantly.

"Very nice," he said. "Did you like it?"

"You were very, very hot," I said, which was the God's-honest truth.

"You're pretty hot, too," he said, still stroking my throbbing dick. I was starting to breathe heavily.

"I'm in this movie," he said suddenly.

"Really?" I said.

"Oh, yeah. The evil dykes always try to show the movies of the guest dancers," he said. "I'm in the next scene."

I thought I couldn't get harder, but I certainly wasn't getting softer.

He leaned over to kiss me, deep, the way we both liked it.

That's when the scene started on the screen.

A behemoth of buff beef was lounging beside a pool with a hard-on the size of a baseball bat.

"We made it in L.A.," José said, which I took to mean the movie.

José was playing the pool boy. He was wearing tiny cutoffs and was rubbing his crotch salaciously while watching the satisfied homeowner fondle his most prized possession.

Their eyes met. José turned and looked me right in my eyes. He was fondling his own crotch as well as mine.

Up on screen he was approaching his employer, who was slathered in oil from head to foot and was glistening in the southern California sun. He spread his legs, putting one foot on the patio stones on each side of the lounge chair he was sprawled on. José slipped off his shorts on the screen and then slipped his sweat pants down to his ankles in the back row of the Gaiety beside me.

"Here?" I said, kind of panicked, my heart beating with fear and anticipation at the same time.

"Nobody will watch us," he said, but I wasn't so sure. I also didn't care.

Movie José was sucking the daddy's dick. Real-life José was on his knees between my legs, pulling my easily opened jeans down off my hips. He had my willing dick in his naturally lubricated mouth right on down to the throat. Up and down he rode in the dark as his image on the flickering screen did likewise.

"God," I said.

"No," he said, stopping his mondo suck job long enough to grin, "it's just me."

"Same thing," I said and he went back to work.

Meanwhile, the brutish brunette had turned his water boy around and was massaging his butt cheeks, which José seemed to know without ever looking at the screen. Because when he turned around, he stood up, leaned his hands on the back of the seat in front of us, and tilted his asshole in my direction. Bluto was playing with starlet José's pretty pucker, and I saw no reason not to join him. I spit on my thumb and started making little concentric circles around his dark asshole, pushing in at the same time.

José was groaning in stereo now, and so were his screen companion and I. I took my cue from José's co-star and put my tongue to his asshole, which was twitching like a sea creature. I was sucking and probing that friendly orifice as greedily as my celluloid counterpart and way more into it than I had ever been before when one of the other members of the audience managed to find his way back to our corner.

"Could you leave us alone?" I hissed at him when I saw him standing there with his hand in his pants.

"It's okay," José said, but pushed the man's hand away when he reached out to touch him.

Up on screen an adorable young slip of a FedEx driver was standing behind an oleander bush watching a gigantic dark-haired hulk poking his dick at the asshole of a breathtaking Latino with a *Keep on Truckin'* tattoo on one inflated bicep.

"I don't have a rubber," I said, beginning to get into it, but José had thought of that, too. Bending over (and backing his sweat- and spit-drenched asscrack against my raging cock) he pulled one out of his sweat pants and handed it to me with a small vial of lube. I cracked the lube open and spread it right onto my target, pushing it inside him with the fingers of my right hand while working the fingers of my left up the knots of his spine while José held his cheeks apart.

When the host of the impromptu pool party started pushing at José's asshole with his safety-sheathed bat, I rolled that condom onto my dick and slid it into as welcoming an asshole as I've ever slipped into. Dark-haired actor-man and I pumped in and out of José. Up on the stage, a thousand Mylar icicles that formed a kind of curtain were reflecting the merciless filmed sunlight of Los Angeles. The FedEx guy had his dick out and at full mast by now, and so did the guy who was watching us at the back of the theater. He made a grab for José's dick, and my neighborly neighbor pushed his hand away.

"No touching," he said insistently to our silent witness, yanking on his own dick with one hand and pulling a nipple nearly off his chest with the other since I had both of my hands on his hips pulling him forcefully onto my dick over and over again. I was Vlad the Impaler and he was an unfortunate prisoner of war.

Up on the screen, the big bad dark guy pulled out of José and let his cum fly.

"You call that coming?" I said out loud, and—in a totally characteristic spasm of competitiveness—I whipped out my dick, ripped off the rubber, put a thumb back in its place, and started jerking to the finish line while my rival's meager cum was shown in slo-mo a half dozen times.

The FedEx man was splashing his joy juice all over his parcel and so was our voyeuristic friend, who was dribbling his own love liquor and making a last grab at José's eggplant-colored dick.

"Would you please give us some privacy?" I said, and José turned around to face me, his dick stretched to the breaking point.

We were slamming our dick-filled fists at our bellies and started to let fly at the same time.

"Oh my GOAWD," I growled back into my throat, not wanting to make a spectacle of myself, and shot clear over José's shoulder and onto the gray presence in the corner.

"Go, baby, go," José was shouting out loud, drawing the attention of every other dancer and client in the place. And because I am an agreeable fuck, I did. I shot more than I ever had before. It was cascading off José's drum-tight torso, and I still kept coming, and then José started to come, and a couple of other gents started circling around and José started screaming "oh…oh…oh…" with each spurt of hot heavy syrup, and the circle of interested observers started tightening and José was nearly convulsive, practically shouting "Give...us...some...privacy...please!"

But I was not at all sure he meant it.

The other men—realizing, after all, that all was, indeed, over—started to disperse. José and I wiped ourselves off with his sweatshirt, pulled our respective clothing back into its recommended configuration for normal use, and cuddled back into our seats.

"Now that," said José, "is what I call sex. A hundred percent."

"Absolutely," I agreed, although just before the film was interrupted for the next dancer, José, his boss, and the grateful FedEx man were swimming around in the pool, paddling into what would doubtlessly be a clumsy three-way. José was licking my neck, totally satisfied, apparently. I felt as if a light bulb had gone on as an idea began to hatch in the incubator of my post-coital mind. I'd have to call Lawrence and see if he was game.

I was on my knees on Lawrence's lovely king-sized bed, my dick buried to the short hairs in his tight, compact ass. He was kneeling, too, his mouth full of José's lollipop. José was on his knees facing me across the small expanse of Lawrence's back. José was working my left nipple with his right hand; I was giving him a bit of loving tit torture with my own. Perhaps because we'd completed the sacred circle, we'd managed to get a lovely rhythm going. The sexual energy was flowing to every inner nook and outer cranny of my body. My ears were red, my asshole clasping and unclasping its own heat as I clenched my ass and leg and stomach muscles with every thrust.

José had just taken my thumb in his mouth when all of us heard a baritone voice somewhere outdoors below us yell "Lights!"—and a million candles' worth of floodlights flicked on outside the window, which was conveniently located next to the rumpled bed. I could see a spring rain falling in the light and behind the clouds the Empire State Building lit up red and green for Cinco de Mayo.

"Camera," the same voice shouted, as José looked at me with grateful glee spreading all over his face.

"And action!"

Lawrence, who was used to the film crew camped outside his building, never missed a beat; José arched his back in total ecstasy, pumping a bit harder into Lawrence's throat; and I kept up my end of the bargain, although I admit I was biting down on my lower lip to keep from breaking out into a roar of laughter. And I did take a peek at our images, flickering on the walls of the apartment like the antics of Javanese shadow puppets. And I did think I caught the faraway sound of a chorus of male voices hooting and woofing and otherwise cheering us on to the finish line as I felt the lava starting to erupt from my buried volcano and a series of earsplitting explosions went off all around us.

Sixteen Degrees of Penetration

Belasco

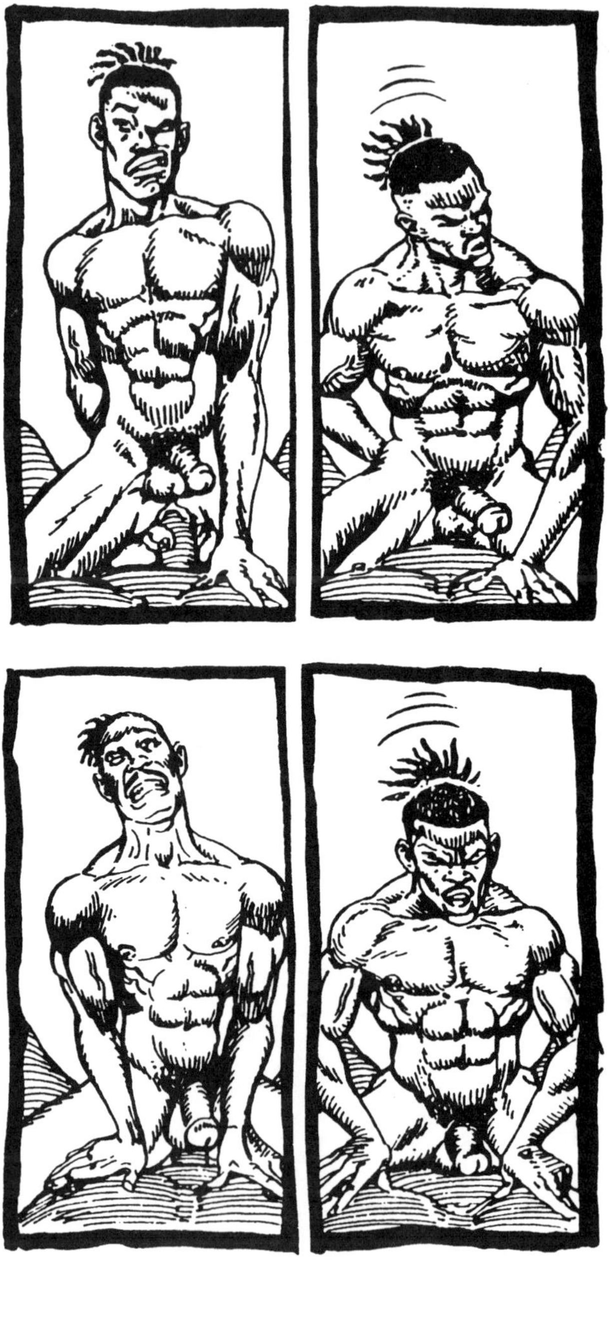

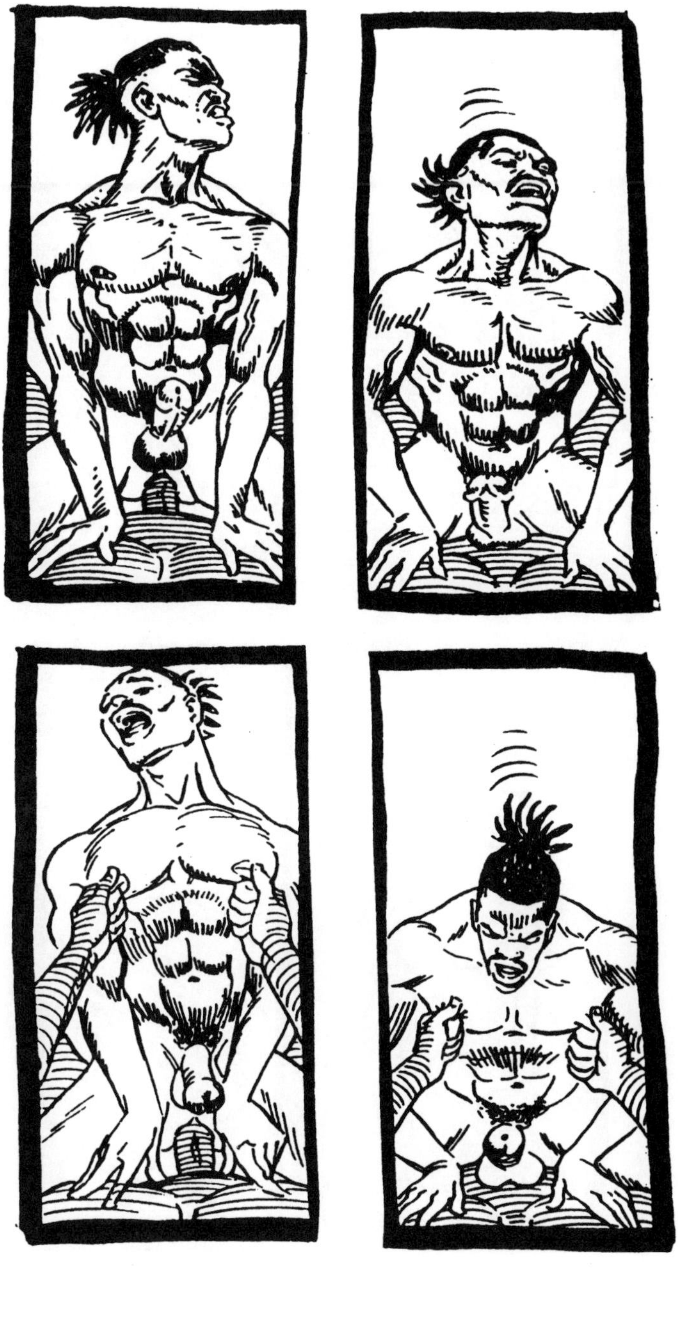

BELASCO ©

Elvis Is Alive and Working On Eighth Avenue

Jameson Currier

I have no doubt that I could have been elected the National Cover Boy for Obsession (and I'm not talking about the Calvin Klein cologne, either). For the truth was, the sad honest-to-goodness-no-bare-bones-about-it truth, I couldn't get Peter out of my mind. He was locked inside my body, infecting every cell he could touch as if he were some kind of yeast-growing herbal resistant bacteria. He had sunburned my skin and blended with my body fluids. He was in my blood, my sweat, my piss, my spit, my hair color. He had become a part of me because of my obsession with him. When someone says he doesn't want you, you only want him more, something that Evan failed to understand in all my moaning and groaning to him. What I didn't want, of course, was another boyfriend to obsess about. One was enough, thank you very much. How could Evan have suggested that I have an affair? An affair wasn't going to make me happy. It was going to make me ballistic, bonkers, ready-to-be-committed-in-a-straitjacket-at-Bellevue. What I needed, I believed, was to find a way to make work what I did already have with Peter.

I will just live with my pain, I decided one afternoon at a temp job where my primary responsibility was to maintain a full pot of decaf coffee for a pair of thick-padded, wide-shouldered, pant-suited-wearing officious Amazons. I had had a full day to just sit and obsess about Peter and watch a coffee machine drip irregularly. I will just make the pain Peter inflicts part of my day-to-day consciousness, I decided. I will make it a part of me. Wouldn't my pain be eased, therefore, because I am aware that it must always be there?

Fuck this, I reconsidered once I had hit the hot pavement on my way home and my mood had become as foul as sour milk. Fuck him. I will just move on. It's over. O-V-E-R. Over! It was mid-June, I remember, and I was walking up Eighth Avenue along that troublesome stretch of the low Forties that resembles what Forty-Second Street between Seventh and Eighth Avenues used to look like years ago before Disney arrived and changed the neighborhood—discount stores, honky-tonk open-door dark bars and neon-enticing, blank window porn shops. It had turned into another unbearably blistering, humid day and I had taken my white dress shirt and tie off and put them in my knapsack and was wearing just a T-shirt with my chinos as I headed uptown. Fuck him. Fuck this job and fuck this city and fuck this starving no-money no-air-conditioner life I had chosen and which kept pulling me down, down, down into the stinking, smelling sewer.

The heat and misery had moved me into a scurrilous mood. That aging bitter dragon lady persona was overtaking my used-to-be-a-happy-go-lucky-chorus-boy personality and it was not a pretty sight. I had nothing to do that night. My apartment was sure to be overheated. I was too broke to see a movie, too broke to even rent a movie if I had been able to watch one in the dusty, sweltering jungle of my apartment. It was too hot to rollerblade, too hot to even try to bike. So I decided to slip into one of the porn shops to cool off for a moment before I faced returning to the Sahara.

Peter, of course, had become my motive for entering the store.

Sure, sure, sure, you might think—wasn't I just another aging guy looking to get his rocks off easily and cheaply? Had I come to that? I had gone to a porn store, after all (it certainly wasn't like I had gone to see one of those outdoor movies in Bryant Park and was hoping to meet someone who had brought along enough picnic supplies to share).

No, no, no, I told the other side of my brain. I was considering buying Peter one of those bootlegged versions of those too-too-buffed West Hollywood gay boy porn tapes when I cashed my next paycheck; it was the only kind I could afford—the Memorexed versions at least—not the real thing—and certainly not the real California experience—and my motive for purchasing this deceptive video version for Peter was that I felt it might smooth over that still nasty-edged memory of our jealous confrontation over the strippers on The Robin Byrd Show. This particular porn store—the one with aisles so narrow you had to shift sideways every time another customer wanted to pass you—was notorious for its less-expensive-than-the-original bootlegged tapes, or at least that's what Evan had led me to believe a few months back when he had confessed to being in my neighborhood, and why he was there.

And so I was standing looking at a shelf of titles, conscious of the dark-skinned attendant looking over my shoulder from some omnisciently high counter, suspicious of my every move—I was trying to read the badly reproduced color photocopies of the original covers which had been slipped behind the plastic sleeve of the black video cases, thinking I might splurge and get Peter one of those Bel Ami or Kristen Bjorn movies—when a tall, slender-framed boy passed behind me. He was wearing bell-bottom jeans, sandals and a blue T-shirt that read Cheers and he had a mop of thick curly sandy blond hair and long sideburns styled as if he were stuck in the 1970s. When I noticed him I thought I had entered a time warp, or, rather, I thought he might have stepped out of one of those ancient high-priced video classics that were shelved behind a locked glass counter underneath the suspicious-minded man-who-thought-I-was-going-to-rip-off-a-rip-off-artist. Unfortunately, the boy disappeared as quickly as it took me to turn sideways and let him pass.

I soon let go of the idea of buying Peter a video, however, when I realized I couldn't even afford one of the bootlegged versions of the bad homemade videocam-and-available-light porn tapes. Then, I grew angry at him for forcing me into feeling as if I owed him a gift because of his inappropriate behavior. He had caused my jealousy, hadn't he? I had every right to be upset. By the time I had made it to the end of the aisle I had worked my mind into the decision that I didn't even want to have a boyfriend, that I would just up and end it with Peter, and as I turned the corner I faced a wall where they were displaying dildos. Maybe I should just get a dildo and give it a name and make it my new boyfriend, I thought. At least he would be there when I needed him. And when I got tired of him I could change his name, put a condom on him and call him someone else, or better yet, just go out and buy another one.

I stood there just looking at the wall. And this wall had it all: there were huge double-headed jelly dongs, super stretch penis sheaths, deluxe super stretch masturbators, latex massage mitts, feelistic flesh-colored plastic supremo dongs with balls, anal balls on a stick, triple ripple butt plugs, inflatable dildos, natural penis extensions, and realistic dildos with a suction cup vase—all with names like Plumber's Delight, The Emperor's Joystick or The Anal Invader.

The tall, thin boy approached the wall and I looked away from the shelf and over at him to let him pass. Instead of sliding behind me he stopped and looked down at me. When I tried to look at him, I realized he was so tall my eyes were level with where his navel was probably located.

"You came to meet Elvis, didn't you?" he asked me, his brown eyes wildly searching out my own, his face leaning so close into mine I could see his acne scars as though they were craters on the moon.

I gave him one of my silly flat-lipped expressions, the kind that just invites anyone to come up and begin a conversation with me, even though I seldom deliver. "Elvis is here?" I asked him.

He motioned for me to follow him, and as I did so I thought, boy, am I dumb, dumb, dumb for doing this. I also knew, however, that at the core of me, what southern-almost-trailer-park-white-trash-boy living in Manhattan could refuse an offer to meet Elvis? Elvis! Elvis is here on Eighth Avenue! It was an experience I couldn't pass up.

I hadn't been to this store in almost a year and as I followed the boy's swishing bell bottoms, we moved through the last aisle and entered a small corridor where cubicles sectioned off with curtains had been built. The boy turned to make sure I was still behind him, then went down a set of dimly lit stairs. I continued to follow him, thinking, well, the joke's on him. I have no money in my wallet if he mugs me. Won't Elvis be surprised? I am poor, poor, poor. Poorer than Elvis ever was. I don't even have a working credit card.

At the bottom of the stairs was a small, shadowy room with a toilet and a sink lit by a low-watt light bulb hanging from a string. The boy peered up and over his shoulder then leaned down and gave me a mischievous smile.

Here it goes, I thought. Here comes the first punch. Just as I was squinting my eyes and tensing my body to lessen the impact of his blow, he unbuttoned the fly of his jeans and slipped his pants below his hips, revealing a pair of white briefs that soaked up all the light the tiny bulb above him could emit. Next he slipped his briefs down over his hips—enough to reveal a thick clump of sandy brown hair at his crotch but not enough to reveal his cock. I thought, well, he must be going to show me a tattoo of Elvis or something. Instead, he slipped his briefs down lower and took out his dick with his fist.

Flaccid, his dick was about as wide as a beer can and about ten inches long. It was an enormous cock which looked shockingly huge against the boy's slender hips and undefined waist, like an industrial strength vacuum cleaner hose attached to a portable dust buster. When the boy pulled his cock out I had to take my eyes away from it and look at his face to make sure he was old enough to own that type of equipment. He met my eyes right away. That look was exactly what he wanted.

"The King," he said, waving his hand down the length of his shaft.

The next thing I knew he was groping my crotch with one hand and stroking his dick with his other. I am not sure where my hands were at that point; possibly they were clasped against my cheeks, as I prepared to howl like McCauley Caulkin in *Home Alone*—because as the boy groped my crotch his dick got bigger and bigger. I know my hands must have ended up there, because at one point I was comparing the length of it against my forearm and trying to decide which one was wider and longer. I was smart enough to know that my own cock should not be revealed. Even with my more than ample regulation equipment I would not even dream about comparing it to this—this huge one. Instead, I felt like a kid who had wandered into a circus freak tent.

Before I knew it, I was on my knees, adrift in the joyous surprise of watching him play with his stunning cock, now at least fourteen inches long and erect, so huge it used up all the space in the room and seemed to pin me captive against the wall. And I could no longer touch it myself; I wasn't interested in sucking on it, wasn't interested in playing with it, had no desire to even consider putting it near my backside. All I wanted was to watch it. I had moved into the combined role of admirer and voyeur—so much so that the boy became self-conscious.

"Take your shirt off," I said to him in a soft, fast whisper.

He grabbed the hem of his shirt and quickly began to remove it.

"No, slower," I said. "Make it sexier."

The boy looked at me, then realized what I had asked him to do.

He pulled his shirt up to reveal his stomach and its light fuzzy line of hair that drifted down from his navel, then lifted it further to reveal his flat, hairless chest, gathering the shirt beneath his armpits while he continued to stroke his huge, beautiful, fleshy hose.

Slowly, now suggestively, he inched the shirt off, then looked down at me for his next cue.

"Stroke your chest," I said.

And he did so.

"Grab the muscle of your chest and then pinch your nipple."

He tilted his head back and smiled, one hand exploring his chest, the other still working his cock.

"Move both hands down to your dick," I said.

He did as I said, swinging his cock as though he were a batter warming up to hit a home run.

"Keep your hips moving."

He tilted his head back again, slacked his knees and did a stationary pelvic dance.

"That's it," I said. There was something miraculous in watching him dance so freely, swaying a cock of that size back and forth. I ran a hand up the side of his rib cage to make sure he was a real person and not some desert hallucination. He shuddered at my touch, as if my fingers were cubes of ice. I could feel his orgasm quivering this high inside him and I watched him cum, pumping his short quick drops into the darkness of the floor.

"Do you want to see me again?" he asked me as he was buckling himself up. I had watched his dick disappear into his jeans and was trying to study the impression that it left against the fabric, but the shadows were, well, creating their own optical illusions.

"Sure," I said, flattered that he would be interested in wanting to see me again. What had I done except provide him with an audience to perform for? I hoped he didn't expect me to pay him. Wouldn't he be surprised to discover that he had just stripped for free? And I hadn't even tried to blow him. "You could drive people crazy with that thing."

"I really get off on seeing people's reaction."

"I would think so," I answered. "You must be very...proud to own something like that."

He smiled back at me and then followed with a torrent of questions as I walked upstairs. Where do I live? (Around the corner.) Is this my first time here? (Is this your first time here?) What do you do for a living? (My occupation is to struggle.)

This last one made him laugh, and as he did so I studied him harder in the brighter upstairs lights of the store. He was remarkably handsome in a Jimmy Stewart stoop-shouldered sort of way, or at least maybe the fact of my knowing what he had to offer made him seem more attractive than he really was. Or, perhaps it was his youth that contributed to his attractiveness. For he had had a boyish enthusiasm during our entire encounter. I, of course, was full of questions for him that I could not dream of asking without seeming like a dizzy old sex-mad queen (how many times a day can you get it up? How many times a day can you get off? Where did you get a dick like that?). Upstairs at the counter by the door, he borrowed a pen from the dark-skinned attendant and wrote his name and number on a scrap of paper. When he handed it to me he said nothing about an amount due for services rendered.

"Elvis," I said, reading his name. Then I introduced myself. "Are you from the South?"

"Memphis," he said. "My mother knew Elvis Presley."

"Really? Did she date him?" I asked, harboring twenty million more unasked questions (Was it the young Elvis or the old Elvis she met? Did she sleep with him? Did she see his dick? Are your dick sizes related?).

"I think so. She doesn't talk much about it."

He followed me out onto the sidewalk, walking so close beside me that his thigh brushed against mine, or, rather, his thigh brushed against my shoulder. I had to take huge steps to keep up with him, or change my pattern to shorter, quicker ones. "How long have you been in the city?" I asked him, feeling as if I had just stepped on a treadmill at a gym.

"A year," he answered.

"Have you done any movies?"

"A few solo scenes," he answered. "My boyfriend doesn't like me doing them."

"Your boyfriend?" I looked up at him after he said this last line, and his face was unreadable, really, though I imagined that he was moving an unseen muscle somewhere forlornly. "How long have you been together?"

"Since college," he answered. "About four years."

"You moved up to the city together?"

He nodded and I stopped walking. We had reached the block I was going to turn down to reach Ninth Avenue and I was once again breathing heavily from the heat and humidity and the exhaustion of the day.

"I can't give it up, though, you know?" he said. He looked at me as if he knew, just knew, I would understand his dilemma, or, rather, that I wouldn't see his dilemma as, well, a dilemma at all. "As long as he doesn't know about it, it's okay."

"It's amazing what you don't know about someone no matter how intimate you are together."

He narrowed his eyes as he took in my words, then exploded them wide. "Yeah," he said, nodding and smiling. "Yeah. But it's not just all about him or me. It's about us. The thing we are when we're together. I love coming home to someone, you know?"

"Yeah," I answered, realizing I had narrowed my own eyes but nothing inside me had exploded in recognition. Instead, I stood there wondering, how did someone so young get to be so lucky and wise, and then mischievously thinking that, well, maybe he thinks with his dick. If that were the case, then he must be a genius.

"It's hard to keep it from being so static," he said.

"Static?" I answered back.

"Sex," he answered, giving me a perturbed look as if my thoughts had wandered away from him, which they had. "Our sex life is nothing like it was years ago."

"And him?" I asked Elvis. "Does it still work for him?"

His smile moved into a frown as he pondered my question. "He doesn't need it as much," he answered. "He's older."

"Aaaaaahhhh," I smiled back at him. "That's when you really need it more. Take my word on it."

He gave me a sure-sure roll of his eyes, as if he really didn't believe my statement. "You're much younger than he is," he said and I was once again flattered, the hideous dragon lady complimented back into being just an aging chorus boy by someone who could describe his genitalia as titanic. And then he stretched his hand out for me to shake.

"Let's get together again," he said.

"Sure," I said, grasping the flesh of him, bonding with him for a final, real moment. "Long live the King," I added. And then he was gone. As I walked away I was smart enough not to glance back to see if he bequeathed me a lingering look. Back in my own mind and my own stride, I realized I had forgotten all about Peter. Maybe Evan was right. Maybe I did need to have an affair to balance my relationship with Peter, or, rather, offset my obsession with obsessing over a man not interested in obsessing over me.

Body Hunger

Grigoris Daskalogrigorakis

I wake up grudgingly a split second before the chirping cricket of my digital time ball, and, by the lack of sound anywhere else, am the first consciousness to rouse in my building. I'm up until dawn the night before waiting for my heart to stop pounding. When I go home late at night and there's no one else around, I try to lie down and nod off, but after a while I start to get the shakes. It's no use. I just can't sleep.

But by daybreak I've usually fallen off. I'm lying in a puddle of my own sweat. This morning, the bedroom is redolent with the smell of rotting gardenias swept into the room by a morning breeze. It's already blistering outside and the sun's begun to singe them. Through the filter of the beginnings of a roaring migraine, the sharp perfume stings my nostrils and excites me at the same time.

It is so difficult to dredge myself out of the torpor of deep sleep and the first crackling pangs of a headache that, half awake, I know I have to resort to the usual solution and I start to pull myself off, languidly at first, the sensation almost too abstract to instigate true arousal, then my heart becomes alert and beats faster, my mind pools and the first identifiable image in it is an oval, blotted in emollient, rubbing against the plate of my midbrain until it soft-focuses into a face, the lambent face of Terence Stamp, the way it looked in the movie Billy Budd.

That visage fades too soon into a profusion of nameless mugs attached to disembodied mouths, loins, napes, cocks, and asses, so dissociated, in fact, that they become mere landscapes of flesh anchored in smell, in spit, in mucous, in the metallic stench of harsh pheromones, all those forbidden particularities and associations I only manage to cut loose from their straitjackets after teen age. Out of that private, heavily-guarded sanitarium, they've turned into detailed, inflammatory things I've made friends of, that I can touch, that wake me up—sort of—during that perfunctory release, squeezing out a few drops of seminal fluid, the sobering up, the "little death" that almost always pulls me out of the "big death" every morning and leaves me distracted now, worrying, still half asleep, wondering for a moment why I'm estranged from women, how repelled I am by the thought that I bear any resemblance to the father I loathe as I look at myself in the bathroom mirror.

But this anxiety rapidly dissolves down the drain. I splash rusty water from the faucet into my eyes, then pull myself back to sitting on the edge of the bed and turn on the TV while I stretch on my socks. There is a local news brief on about summer recreational facilities on the Castaic Reservoir about forty miles northeast of where I am now. But the sight of the gleaming, waterskiing bodies only serves to remind me of the time I am stuck on the nearby "grapevine" on Interstate 5 with a hopelessly debilitated car for eleven hours.

I am driving to San Francisco with three acquaintances. We've just filled up the gas tank, spirits are high, and escape is in the air, when suddenly trucks are playing chicken with my stalled car and passengers on a steep incline as I watch them helplessly in the rear view mirror from the middle lane. Against my pleas, the others vote to stay put until the highway patrol can come to our rescue, but from my privileged position I am seized with such terror watching the transports barely missing us that I can hardly breathe from shaking so violently. Seeing my panic, the others are finally convinced that we're sitting ducks unless we get out. Even having made this decision, it takes fifteen minutes for the convoy of night freight to die down enough for the four of us to sprint to the road shoulder, then clamber up the steep walls of the canyon rising up from the sides of the freeway. Just in time it seems, too, when a passing motorist stops and gives us flares to alert the trucks because the car's hazard lights are too dim to see in the 1:00 A.M. dark. They are all annoyed. I just feel humiliated and disappointed. Two of the other three hitchhike back to the city and take buses to the North.

I am left alone with Billy. We both want to get away this weekend from an emotional parasite that's broken into both our lives and attempted to ransack our souls. The two of us spend the night alone by the roadside rehashing every sequence of events that has led to this crisis of being stranded, every forewarning we've ignored that there was something desperately wrong all along.

It is 104 degrees within a few hours after the sun comes up. Two weeks later my car ends up being abandoned at the turnoff to Magic Mountain amusement park not far from Castaic. Even now, despite the foiled escape and automotive disaster, I can recall with some fondness the mechanic at the auto repair—Jim, a crude, attractive blond man with a moustache, in his early forties, an ex-sailor gone to seed with an anchor tattoo on one arm and a not unattractive beer gut. The mechanic tells me jokingly that my car has had an "aneurysm" as he holds out the small, obscene, thick section of rubber hosing that has burst in the effort to get the old '72 Dodge Dart Swinger up the steep grade. And then I wait here for what seems like hours, days, eras until someone comes to drag me back to L.A. But for the time being I'm stuck in this auto dump with its proprietor, chatting, being attentive to and verbally rough-housing with big Jim, who occasionally calls orders out to his teenage son, learning his daddy's trade at his daddy's knee. Later on I think that it is almost worth having paid $269 and having to abandon the car after all, five miles away, when it overheats again, just to have inhaled that aura, a mixture of axle grease and a day's worth of sweat squeezed out by dry Saugus heat.

For an instant the sight of all the unbridled swimmers and waterskiers on the Castaic reservoir carries me back to the old Athletic Model Guild studios where my best buddy Jack and I went one Saturday night to see a presentation of a friend's male nude photographs for a slick local magazine. He is showing the slides of his shoot because he recruited his models through Physique Pictorial's cornerstone and founder. His series of photos turns out to be part of a monumental slide show that lasts three and a half hours in a makeshift auditorium in the middle of what is an indoor studio with a backdrop against which many of the young male models, who are part of the show, have been captured. The unwitting celebrities of the evening, in fact, can be seen loitering around outside by the pool area in the dark, simultaneously trying to look available and at the same time embarrassed at the impending, shameless display and exhibition of their raw-muscled bodies about to go on inside. I remember the period from the '50s to the mid-'60s when I go to magazine stands and sneak looks in physique magazines, older versions of these bodies, never having either the nerve or the money to buy one.

The evening commences inexplicably with an episode from the TV western "The Rifleman," and a short documentary on FDR. Then the actual slide show begins. The avalanche of images quickly casts an infectious spell of something akin to sexual nausea, but continues relentlessly, lengthens, elongates, extends moistly, a garrulous caterpillar covered with prickles, a clenched forearm alarmed with hair, a profusion of naked men, strays, servicemen, hustlers bent into impossible shapes and positions to facilitate the revelation of their softest and most secret parts to the invading eye of the camera, facing appendages made vulnerable by exposure, lost boys reduced to their uncertain sphincters and fleshy apertures, placed on artificial landscapes as alien as the set of a '50s science fiction film. Sandwiched at random in the midst of this prodigious display of young male animals are occasional summer vacation shots of people recreationally playing in and around the Castaic dam.

The water on the dam swirls into the water in the bathroom sink where I'm poised to piss. In the mildewed room, still dazed, I pull out my dick, stroke it roughly to take the last vestiges of erection out of it so I can piss through it and in the process regard the scar around the glans. For a moment I am assailed by the recollection of my own circumcision with a local anesthetic at the age of ten. My mother takes me and my eight-year-old brother for a routine physical and, at the family doctor's insistence, our genitals are both butchered the following weekend.

Since I am the first, I notice one attending young physician is really cute, an overgrown boy, who winks at me and musses my hair in a gesture designed to put me at ease. This makes me feel especially vulnerable, laid out before him on the operating table, a green cloth draped over my midsection and legs with a hole where my groin is, leaving my generative organs looking wilted and exposed in repose, a wrinkled rubber bath toy awaiting execution. This unfamiliarity with my own body vanishes sharply during the administration of the local anesthetic, six shots of Novocain they inject around my scrotum and the base of my penis. The operation quickly swirls out of control when the surgeon starts to use the scalpel before the anesthetic takes affect. Queasy, yet still alarmed, I lift my head up in time to see blood spurting from the crown of my little prick. For ten days afterward we take stinging pisses through bandages and suffer the humiliation of our mother pulling down our pajamas to show any interested neighbor lady. Perhaps what she is really trying to show them is to what lengths she is willing to go to make her family fit into its adopted culture. I look at this indelible mark of Cain and

Abraham and recognize the trace of its scar as the same one I have seen stamped on hundreds of fellows fallen beside me, especially when I can feel the pulsations of their heads and hearts throb within my clenched fist and swollen lips.

Disoriented and dizzy, I stumble and stagger into the kitchen and realize that I probably won't successfully shake the fog out of my head until I'm in the street and on my way to work. Just out of my sight, on the periphery of my vision at the edge of the kitchen table under a pile of newspapers, I spot an SX-70 of what looks like a mound of meat. I vaguely remember a night when I suggest to a friend that we finish a pack of film taking portraits of each other, then tease and torture the pigment into distorted phantasms of ourselves that reduce us to caricatures out of *Gargantua* and *Pantagruel*, beings escaped out of a Rabelaisian universe, refugees from the grotesque, reproductive body of the mother.

I casually rifle through the small pile of picture cards and discover it's a close-up I took of my lost friend Scott who was visiting Los Angeles for a week at New Year's three years ago. The color is bad, all monochromatic and red, making Scott's head look like a fruit and his complexion ruddy. In real life he has coal-black hair and green eyes and skin as translucent as egg shells. I have known Scott now for twelve years.

After the summer I first meet him I don't see Scott again for nine years. Scott joins the Air Force. I get one or two letters a year, even for the five years Scott is stationed in Germany. When he comes back to the United States to the Army/Navy language school in Monterey, Scott contacts me and we renew our acquaintance. Scott is a tall, lanky, sensitive man, obsessed with playing the piano and with the possibility (but not the actuality) of having a fulfilling relationship with a woman. Except for Scott's obsession with the piano, this makes him different from me only in the gender designation of the peculiar form of his desire. Years later, right before he vanishes from sight, Scott miraculously meets, has an affair with, and marries a schizophrenic woman, the perfect recipient for Scott's vast, untapped resource of love.

One night the two of us take a number of SX-70s of each other, squeezing the color in some of them afterwards until the light streams from the beacons of our head holes and orifices, two subjects made out of vibrating shafts of light, although one I take of Scott has the clarity of one of Caravaggio's boys. "We should exhibit these in the Louvre," Scott suggests, laughingly. A Pre-Raphaelite Saint Sebastian, I think, as I gaze at the Polaroid of Scott—an etiolated martyr carved in marble.

It's been two years, almost three, since I lost track of Scott. I even try the Air Force Locator but am given the whereabouts of another airman with Scott's name instead. I never follow it up. After Scott comes and visits me from the Air Force base in Monterey that time, he calls me up long distance afterward and tells me he would have liked to have had an affair with me but is too afraid to because of his position in military intelligence. This information comes out of the clear blue sky and knocks me absolutely speechless. It turns into fantasy stuff for me in the following years, especially once, in the steam room of a bath house in Toronto, surrounded by young men of British ancestry, where I fancy that the towels must really be Irish linen and that Scott's peeking at me through every cloud of steam, or from just behind every booth door in the toilet.

There is a lesson in futility to be learned here but I adamantly refuse to learn it. The day before Scott returns to Monterey, I take him to the barber to have his already short hair made even shorter to conform with regulation length. The whole time I just sit in a chair leafing through a stack *of Field & Streams* and *True Detectives*, half turned on by the smell of Scott's dirty socks a few feet away, which lingers acridly on the periphery of my attention. How much nicer, I think, it would be to be sitting in one of those ubiquitous Charles Eames chairs in an airport on the way to Germany with Scott rather than on this torn vinyl bench at the barber's. At the bus depot Scott asks me to button the hard-to-reach button behind the collar of his white Brooks Brothers shirt. Task accomplished, I slip my hand momentarily around Scott's neck in a caress. Right before Scott boards the bus I embrace him impulsively. There has been no physical precedent for this. Scott is caught off guard and his eyes tear in response. He doesn't even attempt to hide it, I notice, surprised, as he disappears into the bus. Scott is the kind of guy, possessed of such profound empathy, that later he seduces and has an affair with a friend of his who has grown suddenly suicidal, to keep him from killing himself, and it works.

The sequence of thought that's led to Scott weighs heavily on me. What might have been, if only—you could waste your whole life in such idle conjecture, such vain contemplation. I flop back onto the bed. "Oh hell, work can wait another hour," I mutter to myself. Thoroughly distracted now, I idly pick up a *Time* magazine to the right of the mattress. In an article about the Vatican Exhibit at the Metropolitan Museum in New York I am reminded of the vandalism of the Pieta years ago and of the effigy of the boy and his mother, that limp masochist across the nurse's lap. The only way I am going to get Scott out of my system, I realize now, is to masturbate again, and it doesn't take long to pull a few pertinent figments out of that visual generic pool of melted lubricant and congealed hearts and sketch them with something resembling desire.

This is how it goes: me, I am clad in a pair of shredded BVDs (the twentieth century loincloth), a torn T-shirt and black Banlon socks that have seen better days, propped up on a rough-hewn throne of marble. Scott, barely conscious, is draped over my lap and in my arms in nothing but his Jockey shorts, dying, ostensibly. Although it's a daunting task, I gratefully attempt to soothe him as best I can with my hands, eventually annihilating my mouth somewhere in the vicinity of the elastic selvage of Scott's underwear, the upsurge at at the apex of my thighs pushing up into

Scott's back—one martyr dying, lying on another martyr's lap—a latter day Pieta for a new age and another picture for me to file away in my image repertoire. The formality of this eroticized psychodrama rapidly deteriorates into something less solemn and more frantic. For a fleeting moment, and only ephemerally, I am disturbed by the possibility that none of this fantasy is particularly correct politically, but I quickly dismiss that thought with a stroke of my hand. A few dry spasms are summarily achieved and my brain is flooded with beta-endorphin-induced nothingness, relief and remorse. I file away this series of icons lovingly for later, instant replay.

Unable to procrastinate any longer I pull myself out of my overwhelming inertia and get dressed. As I put on my coffee-stained work pants and green and pink flower shirt, I play my current favorite song on my pre-hi tech record player. I've been playing it to death lately, trying to suck as much pleasure out of it as possible—a dirge in which the vocalist's plaintive wailing insists that "...you don't give me love, you give me pale shelter." If the truth were told, I realize, I have hardly ever been in the position to voice such a complaint legitimately except in theory because there's never been a willing, appropriate "you." But somehow it manages to strike a sympathetic chord nonetheless. On the way to work the radio in my car plays another song by the same group. "This is going to be some day," I mumble to myself, my headache radiating into clusters of stabbing pain behind my right eye. I decide that it's not just "body hunger," as my ex-friend Pam calls it, that gives me the shakes at night, but an ache that's deeper and more difficult to define or relieve. I pat my groin and realize that the soreness I feel there is due to too much agitation so early in the day. But I can be sure that by dawn of the next morning there will no longer even be a vestige of this present ache.

Puppy Love

Jeff Kirby

"Wanna play catch? You game?"

He pants—whimpers.

"Good puppy! Now let's just move my jock over to the side. There you go! Don't touch it, not yet, just look at it. Study it, yeah, look at the power puppy, nice big boner for you to slobber. Watch me flex...wait, look. Whoa, yeah, look at that. Look how it bobs and twitches in front of your face. Yeah. You like that, puppy, you're my puppy, you're such a good boy! Give me a kiss, yeah, that's my boy. What's that? You want my jock, you want it? Here it is, here you go, boy. Fetch! Go get it, go get it. Bring it back here. Good puppy. Here, boy. Let me have it. Here, here, bring it here."

"Grrrrrrrr."

"Let it go."

"Grrrrrrrr."

"Yeah, yeah, you love that jock, don'tcha boy! Whoops! Where'd it go, boy, find it. Go find it. Oh, you think I still have it, do you? Smart puppy. Look. Look, here it is! No. No. Sit. Stay. I said stay. Don't move. Good boy. I'm gonna hang these straps off my dick.

Yeah, it's okay. I understand."

I grip my dick, circle it around the kid's mouth, smack it into my palm. "Stay," I command the kid, and then I release my dick. It slaps my stomach. The kid goes crazy.

"What? What do you want, puppy? Oh, you want that big drop of pre-cum, don'tcha? Yeah, look at it hang there. Whew, yeah, open your mouth. Stick out your tongue. Pant. C'mon, boy, pant. Let me hear you. What's that? Speak! Speak! That's my boy. Good pup! Just a lick. Just that drop. There you go."

The kid, so obedient his tongue barely swipes the head of my prick, expertly retrieves his reward. A strand of fluid connects us. I flex my cock. The fluid cord breaks.

"Remember how to play catch? Good boy. Go get your leash!"

He should remember. Catch is basically me swinging my dick in front of his face, while he's tied to a radiator trying to reach for and catch the head in his mouth. I won't let him touch it until I see his entire body strain for a taste. Usually he's beet-red, eyes bulging, in a puddle of sweat. The kid loves it. Last time, he popped his lips off my prick for nearly an hour before I shot in his face. Better make sure his water dish is fresh.

"What's the matter, you're not tired, are you, puppy? Reach for it."

After ten minutes, I'm bored. I'm standing as close as I can to his lips. Just a fraction out of reach, bobbing my dick ever so slightly to coax his tongue that extra inch to release. The kid's working hard and is hard as a rock himself. I discipline him to take breaks, lap up some water, build up gradually, not wear himself out too fast. I know it's work, believe me. I did my own strict time as a cock slave puppy. But it shouldn't be all work. It should be pleasurable, unpredictable, exhilarating. Time to change the game.

"Do you wanna be a puppy? Or do you wanna be my baby boy?"

Ah, just as I thought. The kid loves being a big baby for my big dick. I first clued into this when he started gurgling over the

We've been meeting on and off for a couple of years now. I'd say he's about thirty-six, probably in business, maybe design. He says he loves what we do together. Means a lot to him. He'd like to "go public"—serve me in front of a group of guys, in a toilet perhaps—that is, if I think he's good enough. I like his devotion.

The kid's mouth is wide open, determined—with a look I've never seen before—a mix of joy and panic, as he starts to fall.

Blueboy

Kelly McQuain

Sometimes he thinks the ringing exists in his ears—a lingering symptom. But shrill waves of sound rise above engines idling outside. The noise billows yellowed curtains and cracks the plaster walls of this third-story walk-up. As the pay phone rings on the street corner below, Michael cradles his own phone against his ear and knows he is haunted.

The old rotary receiver in his hand is heavy enough to crack a skull. Once, years ago, Michael considered using it for that purpose. A trick from the Bike Stop had gotten too rough—biting Michael's back, drawing blood. Michael lay pressed facedown against the mattress, hands pinned hard against his spine, helpless beneath the weight from above. As the trick rode him harder, Michael fought to free himself. He wanted to grab the phone off the nightstand and clobber the creep. Wanted to smash the son-of-a-bitch's brains, kick him out the door and down the stairs till his sorry ass spilled into the street.

But Michael's wrists were locked, he couldn't. Compliance lay imbedded deep inside him, a wanting to let go that he muffled like a scream. His struggling slackened. As the trick bit flesh, Michael bit his own tongue. He pictured his father standing in the room watching in disgust.

Later, it became difficult for Michael to pick up tricks from bars—even second-choice psychos—so he invited home hustlers from the corner. Never mind that sex was no longer transformative, a means of forgetting himself and existing only as a body. Each tryst ground him down like a face mashed into a mattress. Still the urge remained.

When a hustler tried to make off with his weed and rent money, Michael lashed out with rage long-held, his fists as fierce as any man-made weapon. For days he nursed bloody knuckles, fantasized about knocking the hustler's teeth in with the phone receiver, twisting the cord around the guy's neck and teaching him a lesson—until the fantasy produced such a hard-on that Michael grew sick of himself.

At least the Blueboy had never ripped him off. The Blueboy, with his chipped front tooth and stained T-shirt—a cornflower hue matching his eyes, fabric loose on a frame not yet full. The boy was slim-shouldered but large-footed, his body unsure what part should first surge to adulthood. He stood nervous and shivering beneath a white-blue circle of streetlight, kicking the curb in a pair of dirty Air Jordans that Michael would have thought stolen had the kid been any other hustler. But this one hadn't been on the street long enough for his home clothes to wear out—just long enough for the Indian Summer to turn, and him without a coat.

Michael had been walking home from a 24-hour convenience store that October night. Across from his building at 17th and Pine, traffic slowed past a parking lot where hustlers gathered, their lean forms illuminated by the red blink of the E-Z Lot sign flashing overhead. Michael watched the young men preen, teasing the cars that circled the asphalt island. Middle-aged men sizing up aging kids. Lost boys leaning toward open windows. Sharks and prey, but which was which?

As the hustlers bartered feigned innocence, the new kid standing off a ways caught Michael's eye. The boy studied the stance of the regulars, trying to figure out what to do, looking as scared of the cars as he was in need of them.

Michael shifted the bag of groceries in his arms and passed the young man slowly. The kid latched on to Michael's unsubtle once-over, returned it. Asked to bum a smoke, his voice straining to produce a huskiness Michael knew wouldn't last into the next sentence.

A long time ago Michael had quit taking offense at hustlers' assumption that he needed to pay for sex. Now, with his recent lay-off, it pleased him to look like he could still afford to. He stood up straighter, wedged his groceries under one arm and gave the kid a cigarette. He set his bag at his feet and lit one for himself, cupped his hand around the flame as the kid leaned in close for a light, the match illuminating the near colorlessness of the boy's hair and the clear skin of his features. Michael studied him—mouse-eared but sweet-lipped, nose a blunt, boyish wreck. The kind of face that would always look young, and for all the wrong reasons.

The boy drew hard, his cigarette finally catching as the match burned low against Michael's fingertips. Michael quickly tossed the match away and blew on his singed skin, embarrassed.

Want to party? The boy's voice cracked.

Michael nearly laughed. But he had struck out earlier at two separate bars and wasn't in the mood for anymore bullshit. He sighed and confessed the truth. *I'm broke.* His gin-and-tonic grin did the apologizing for him. He shrugged and pointed across the street. *Live over there. Got a couple joints upstairs. Half a bottle of gin.* He picked up his groceries again. *Eggs, doughnuts, juice. Want to party? Be my guest.*

Without waiting for an answer, Michael stepped into the street, his path a slanting beeline toward his door. A car honked, and Michael flicked his half-finished cigarette at the guy's windshield.

His key was in his lock when the Blueboy called out from behind.
Okay.

Unlike other tricks, the Blueboy let Michael fuck him. That the kid went for that, even for no money, proved he wasn't a typical hustler. Just a lonely gay kid like Michael had been years ago. Or maybe, thought Michael, the boy simply enjoyed charity work. Who cared, though, about what lay inside a hustler's heart? The part Michael was interested in lay a few organs lower.

Michael knew to be careful, ever since the day the woman at the clinic confirmed his worst fear. The bad news had coiled in his gut, snaking up to bite his heart. It was the same mix of fear and helplessness he had known as a child when a bird had fallen from a tree into the sandbox where he drove his Matchbox cars. The creature's wings gray and molting, its eyes a milky white. Michael threw down his cars, gathered the trembling thing in cupped hands, and ran for his mother. His mind was already bedding a shoebox with soft cotton, seizing the tiny dropper used for his baby sister's medicine, wondering what to fill it with to save so tiny a life. Hopes of rescue were dashed when Michael's mother knocked the bird from his hands, its hollow bones colliding against the porch steps. She shook Michael by the shoulders. *Look at your hands.* Crawling with tiny orange spiders from the diseased bird, the insects' legs prickling pinpoints that moved over Michael's skin. Inside, the water scalded as she made him scrub flesh pink, then pinker. She pinned his wrists against the white porcelain and poured rubbing alcohol across the rawness, reddening Michael's fingers and palms to flames. Her worry his now. All afternoon, all evening, Michael afraid to touch his face, his hair, lest contamination creep into the parts of him he knew not how to protect.

But now, alone with the Blueboy, Michael pushed the memory away, rolled on a condom then rolled on top, letting his weight sink the kid's shoulders deep into the bed. The Blueboy lifted his feet and locked them behind Michael's head.

Michael tried to lose himself in their closeness. Inside the Blueboy, he felt powerful and sure. His hands skimmed the subtle scallop of the boy's ribs, skin cool to the touch but warming as blood moved fast beneath. Michael liked the feel of the boy below, the tickle of leg hair along his sides, its silken floss. Michael pushed harder.

When Michael woke the next morning, the Blueboy was gone. Michael rose and latched his door, walked to the kitchen. An empty container of orange juice sat on the counter. A faint sprinkling of confectioner's sugar snowflaked the cutting board by the sink. Michael opened his fridge to find his box of Pepperidge Farm doughnuts half empty. Eggs untouched, Stroehmann loaf twist-tied tight. Michael looked in his cookie jar for the last of his cash and his stash. Both still there.

A month later, Michael saw the Blueboy again. The kid had shown up hours early for the night trade, and sat smoking cigarettes atop the low brick ledge that walled in the E-Z Lot across from Michael's building. Michael was coming back from the pharmacy, a bag full of pills and herbal tea tucked into the pocket of his jacket. The headlights of a Saturn leaving the lot flickered across the kid's features, leaving them aglow in the waning autumn light. The *black-and-Blueboy* this time—the kid's left eye a swollen shiner that made Michael wince in sympathy.

What the hell happened? he asked.

The kid shrugged.

Michael sat down beside him. *I never got your name last time.*

The kid twisted his mouth into a sneer. *What do you want it to be?* All pretense, though; Michael could see tears welling up in his mismatched eyes.

Michael sighed. *Want some tea?*

Michael got the kid's story that night, though never his

name. He remained the Blueboy, though with a few details sketched in: since the death of his parents in an expressway car crash, he had lived with his older brother and sister-in-law in the family house in Devil's Pocket, a rough ramshackle neighborhood in south Philadelphia tucked along the Schuylkill River. The kid had become homeless, however, at the end of summer when his brother discovered his journal. A guidance counselor had urged the Blueboy to use it to write out his feelings about his parents' accident. But soon the journal became a reservoir for other things—drawings of a boy in English class, experimental sonnets. Each entry grew bolder than the last as ambiguous plural pronouns gave way to "he's" and "him's"—incriminating words that signified a handsome jock the Blueboy had a crush on. The journal had chronicled the Blueboy's soul until his brother found it, screaming how it pissed on the memory of their mother and father, a point he drummed in with fists.

The Blueboy had no choice but to run away. For a while after the weather got cold, his sister-in-law slipped him in the back door come nightfall, let him hide in the cellar behind the water heater. But two days ago the Blueboy's brother had found out, gave them both a beating they wouldn't soon forget.

Some iced part inside Michael cracked and slid free upon hearing the story. The stranger's words awakened images of his own father. The last time Michael had seen him alive was the summer following his sophomore year of college. An older man Michael had met at a Jersey mall kept calling the house, prompting Michael's father to ask point blank whether his only son was a faggot. Michael had snapped *yes*, the word blade-sharp on his tongue. The only thing that saved Michael from a trip to the emergency room that day was the sudden wail of his mother standing in his open bedroom door. Both Michael and his father froze as the small woman jerked her head forward then flung it back against the doorjamb again and again in a vain effort to beat her son's confession from her brain.

Now Michael's father had lain dead two years from a burst coronary. At his sister's request, Michael had gone to the funeral held at the old Catholic church where he had once been an altar boy. He felt underdressed in his jeans and wool blazer, and his general lack of sympathy. He was shocked to see how old his mother had grown since he walked out of her life, no light in her eyes as she stiffened inside his hug. When Michael's sister invited him home after the service, Michael had nodded, *Sure*. But he had come by train and felt awkward asking relatives he hadn't seen in years for a lift. No one offered. In the end he walked the half-mile back to the station alone and returned to the city without telling his mother and sister good-bye. In the month that followed, Michael's sister called three times, offering Pollyanna clichés: *time to heal, make a fresh start, let bygones be bygones.* But she and her husband now lived in Florida; distance produced détente, but not a truce.

Michael pushed his family from his head, concentrated on the boy sitting on his bed blowing steam off his second cup of whiskeyed chamomile. Lamplight from the nightstand colored the boy's bruised eye deep violet. Beautiful, Michael thought. He reached out, ran his finger across the wound. The boy flinched at the contact. Blue eyes skirted Michael's own, wide black pupils brightening to iced ultramarine.

The Blueboy exhaled slowly, fear of violence passing. He rubbed a drop of tea spilled on his denims. Michael sat down on the bed. His fingertips brushed the hair above the kid's ear. The bruise was a continent Michael could lose himself in, the boy a body welcoming comfort.

Michael wanted to weigh their needs against each other's, but no scale existed for such things. Senses took over, bending him forward, brushing his lips over the boy's smoother set. No need to explain himself, his father, the virus in his blood. His body its own obvious motive.

Michael pulled back to steady his senses. In the brief moment it took to set their teacups by the phone, words pushed up inside him. He wanted to tell the Blueboy he was sick inside, perhaps always so. But when he turned back, the Blueboy was already pulling his shirt over his head, dropping it to the floor, a mixture of desire and resignation on his face.

The sight of the boy bare-chested and blooming stole the breath from Michael's lungs, drowned confession's slim second chance. Michael shoved the Blueboy down, worked his fingers into the grooves of the boy's ribs, clutching smooth skin. The kid's eyes glazed over then flickered shut, arms reaching for the headboard.

The boy's flawed beauty astounded Michael. Something tight loosened inside him, but it wasn't love, Michael wouldn't let it be. The thought saddened him. He drew a slow breath, amazed that his body was capable of even deeper vulnerabilities than illness. He swallowed hard and shivered.

Inside Michael's gut, desire curled—a ball of cottonmouths. He pulled off their clothes, hooked the Blueboy's legs over his shoulders. A part of him wanted to slide red and raw into the boy's ass, shoot those cottonmouths deep. But blood and sperm, especially his, couldn't offer such communion. He rolled on a condom, and again, another.

Less resistance this time. The Blueboy bit his lip, scrunched his eyes in his damaged face, his body not yet fully broken in. His ass, rhythmic and ringed, clenched the shaft of Michael's cock. Perhaps if Michael fucked the Blueboy hard enough, he could lose himself inside the kid. He didn't want to think his own thoughts anymore. He wanted to rip off layered latex and feel his body let go, regardless of the consequence. The boy bucked, like he wanted to come but couldn't. Michael's fingers squeezed the kid's shoulders hard enough to leave marks. He hunched forward, found the head of the kid's dick and tongued it to his mouth. The Blueboy gasped, body convulsing. Michael pushed harder and felt the tension in his gut uncoil, shooting up and out.

Michael swallowed the last of the Blueboy's come, then let the still-hard cock fall from his mouth. He pulled out, gently lowered the boy's legs to the bed, then removed sodden condoms and tossed them into a waste basket. He settled his head on the Blueboy's stomach. The kid's breathing slowed; his legs trembled.

Michael felt the boy's hand run over the crown of his head where his hair was thin. *Awesome*, the Blueboy whispered.

Michael wanted to laugh but couldn't. He rolled over and swallowed the Blueboy's cock again, apparently sending an electric jolt through the boy's spent nerves. The Blueboy said nothing as Michael lay there, tongue circling the sensitive shrinking head.

The next morning, Michael cooked them an elaborate breakfast. His new AIDS Buddy, Keith, had taken it upon himself to keep Michael's refrigerator well stocked, and Michael was glad for the healthy appetite of company. The Blueboy ate greedily, his hair wet from the shower, his bruise a green copper-stain in the morning light. Michael's own food grew cold on his plate, his appetite only for the pleasure his eyes drank in. He tore an ATM receipt in half and wrote his phone number on the part not showing his deficit, then handed it over. *Come see me again*, he said. The Blueboy shrugged and put on his coat.

When the first call came at 3 am, Michael stirred from sleep and groggily pressed the cold phone to his ear. It took a long moment to decode the "*It's me*" at the other end. More words, a whisper, a bare exhale of breath. *Look outside*.

Michael gathered an extra handful of cord and pulled the phone to the window. He squinted down at the snow-slushed street. In the watery light of the street lamp, a figure stood by the pay phone. The caller's face turned up toward Michael's window like a swimmer surfacing for air. The Blueboy. Michael breathed in deep at the sight.

While the Blueboy choked through the latest fight with his brother, Michael kept the receiver tucked against his ear and scrambled to find clean clothes. It had been days since he'd last been out of his robe. Quickly he pulled on jeans and slipped on a shirt. Before the kid's quarter ran out, Michael took down his number, scribbling it on the wall above his nightstand. He ran a washcloth over his face and called right back.

Even with his window closed, Michael heard a faint ring from the street below before the kid picked up the phone. As the Blueboy confessed he had nowhere else to go, Michael walked to the window again and saw the kid's face still tilted up toward his window. Michael told him he'd throw down his keys.

Soon, any late hour "*It's me*" was all it took for Michael to let in the Blueboy. No sad tale of brother and fists required. Few words at all; the language of bodies simply enough.

With Keith's help Michael kept his apartment cleaner—clothes put away, papers off the couch—as if expecting company. When Keith asked why, Michael revealed nothing. The Blueboy had to be kept secret, the one thing Michael could look forward to now when every doctor visit meant plummeting T-cells. Keith would ask too many questions—were they having safe sex, did they know the risks involved? Though Michael was careful, he knew Keith would consider skirting the issue a sin of omission. But surely the Blueboy knew, didn't he? Surely he noticed Michael's sallow cheeks, the skin growing thin on his frame.

In shame, Michael waited for nights of freezing rain or heavy snowfall. Always the Blueboy called from the pay phone on the street below, always after Michael had gone to bed, the sharp ring of the old black rotary jarring away dreams unremembered.

But most nights Michael lay alone, listening to his body: neck vertebrae clicking against a pillow's imperfect comfort. Blood pulsing in his ears. If he slept at all, it was only to dream about rising to go to the bathroom, on his way looking out his window at the corner below, the snow-sludged street empty of all but the lost boys and the lost men who fed them.

When the Blueboy came again, Michael didn't want to undress.

He didn't want the Blueboy to see his mongrel-thin frame, elbows and ribs ready to tear through faint skin. A cold wind raged outside as the Blueboy insisted; he lay in bed already naked, erect, wanting the heat of skin to warm him. He tugged off Michael's shirt, and the blue sky in his eyes clouded over.

Words had gotten bigger the longer left unsaid. Michael watched the Blueboy slowly roll to the side, making room for him to lay down. Michael sagged against the mattress, reached out and cupped shrunken fingers around the boy's crotch. He lowered his head and leaned in open-mouthed. The Blueboy's hand stopped him. *You don't have to.* The kid's erection was flagging. *Let's just hold each other.*

Michael turned from the pity in the boy's eyes. The Blueboy tried to spoon around him but Michael shrugged him off. He couldn't stand the feel of the kid's stare lasering his back. Michael clenched his teeth and focused his eyes on his nightstand, on the phone heavy enough to kill someone, its black plastic limned with moonlight, the silence of the room looming louder than any bell.

Michael grew to hate the Blueboy, his good looks and health, the pity and shame in the boy's blue eyes. Rage circulated through Michael's system. It stooped his shoulders, gnawed his gut, leeched oxygen from his blood. It consumed the meat of cell after cell as it shrank his body and the size of his heart.

Keep your spirits up, Keith said every visit, bringing prepared food from an AIDS organization now. Michael ate a few mouthfuls while Keith offered health tips Michael would never heed, his pretense of hospitality wearing threadbare. After Keith left, Michael flushed the rest of his meal down the toilet, watched it swirl away with the water.

When the Blueboy called again, Michael said he was too sick to see him. It was true; he lay curled in the mess of his bed, the phone receiver a black dumbbell crushing his ear. Couldn't even beat off anymore to the other *Blueboys*—dog-eared magazines stacked inside his steamer trunk. Forget someone real. No rallying himself for a kid who was only a hustler, who asked for more than money or marijuana, who asked on a cold winter night to steal through walls better left in place.

On the phone, the Blueboy's voice choked through tears. *It's snowing. I'm cold. She snuck me in the basement again, but he heard us. I think my nose got broke.*

Sickness puddled in Michael's bed, assaulting his senses. He couldn't even walk to the window now. *I can't help you,* he rasped.

You're just like him!

The Blueboy's words felt like blows inside Michael's brain. With great effort Michael carefully returned the receiver to its cradle.

Outside, snow howled.

Keith came the following morning, cleaned the bed's caked filth, and taxied Michael to Graduate Hospital. There, doctors probed Michael's stick-figure frame, pumped his veins full of drugs and fluid, and snaked tubes down his throat to ease air into lungs. They started him on a new combination therapy they called a cocktail, as if such a name could invent for Michael pleasant memories of Boatslip tea dances and Fire Island free-for-alls.

That week in the hospital, Keith brought Michael piles of magazines and newspapers to read to "keep his spirits up." Michael grew sick of Keith's good intentions and had no choice but to rally. By Friday he was cleared to go home.

Waiting for Michael's release forms, Keith read aloud week-old headlines. *Space shuttle snafu, Main Line murder stumps DA, teenager's body washes up by Schuylkill refinery.* The last sent a chill down Michael's spine.

The details Keith offered were imprecise: runaway from Webster and Bambrey found drowned the morning of January 2, discovered by a Blackmoore Chemicals employee. Police believed the seventeen-year-old jumped or fell from either the South Street or Walnut Street Bridge. Relatives reported no note or precipitating factor other than depression following the recent loss of close family members. The body had been lodged in the chemical company's filtering system among snow and ice dumped into the river following recent storms. The name of the minor was not released.

The Blueboy, Michael was sure. He wanted to crawl back in his hospital bed, have the nurse kick out Keith and nail shut the door, let him die in peace. The Blueboy's face floated before him: pale hair falling across forehead, icy depths of his eyes, the kissable crook of his nose. Heart full of as much tragedy as any Michael had ever endured. And now lost. Now dead.

Back home, Michael listened patiently to Keith's schedule of when to take what medication. Keith taped a reminder to Michael's refrigerator, and before leaving went over the instructions for working the electronic alarm on Michael's new pocket pillcase. When he was finally alone, Michael flushed his medicine down the toilet, dropped the plastic case in the trash, then opened every window in the house to the cold outside.

Let the grave take him. He phoned Keith's answering machine and told his AIDS Buddy not to bother delivering meals anymore; he was feeling so well he had decided to visit his sister in Tampa, and would stay through winter if the sun proved kind. Michael didn't mention that he hadn't spoken to his sister since his father's funeral, that he was merely trying to buy enough time to die quietly. Hanging up, he looked around his room at all the things he wouldn't miss and imagined Keith or the landlord finally finding him, his thin carcass beached on a tangle of bedcovers.

Fever retook him. Michael lay swirled in sweaty sheets. Half-dead in dreams, he felt himself slip free of his body. All around him darkness stretched, as vast and black as space. Glints of light flickered high above like stars. But Michael was far away from them and any warmth they possessed. He felt something cold and awful clamp tight around him, surrounding him in a second skin. Michael knew it was the Blueboy's corpse, still wet from the river, sealing over him like a wound closing.

They were together now.

Michael stared out through the boy's dead eyes, and watched powerless as the Blueboy's stiff limbs, now his own, stumbled against the engulfing dark. His arms and legs tried to climb to the stars, but they lay out of reach across an impossible distance. Could angels even scale such heights, wondered Michael, surrounded by the dead boy's wet decay, feeling the leaden hope in the Blueboy's heart.

From distant rifts light bled down. The faint penumbra illuminated faces Michael had known in life. Men who had died of the same disease from which he was now dying. Their deaths had left them with scarecrow-limbs and bodies shrunken to bone-bag forms, stretched skin a gray afterthought. Their funeral-stitched lips did not move, yet Michael heard their soft susurrant chorus building inside his head, their yearning for life and light.

With great effort, these bodies slowly pulled themselves heavenward. But such fear among them. Trembling fingers found desperate purchase in nooks willed from nothing. The stars of life shone sweet and distracting as each body struggled higher. *Do not forget me*, minds called. Michael felt their silent yearning seek him out. Could the Blueboy hear it too?

With sudden strain the Blueboy joined the ascent, up past starlit windows that revealed a brick row home, snowy streets, car doors opening to strangers. A flash of fists, a rush of water. Who would want to go back to that?

Hand over hand the Blueboy climbed, up a faint thread heretofore invisible. It dangled from a rift in the firmament. It disappeared inside the Blueboy's chest. Michael felt it, silky and gossamer thin, snaking around his essence, drawing tight.

Do not forget me.

Much closer now, lit windows seared the cold blue eyes masking Michael's own. The Blueboy's rough hands pulled both their bodies through one blinding laceration. On the other side, wind-snapped curtains revealed a new perspective: a dark room where walls shrank toward familiar vanishing points. Where a messy bed floated in the chilled blue air. And atop a damp mattress lay the rafted figure of a dreaming man.

Michael woke, somehow finding the strength to shut his window. Then he searched the bathroom for extra medicine Keith might have squirreled away. No luck. He fished the empty pill bottles from his wastebasket and set out to refill them at the 24-hour CVS drugstore.

The clock by the phone glowed 12:15 a.m. as Michael fled his apartment. Coatless, he stumbled through Philadelphia's Rittenhouse Square, past a dry fountain and beneath bare branches silvered with snow. Flakes swirled around him as he reached out toward passersby, groping for handholds among the living. The strangers recoiled.

Still he managed to make it to the store at 19th and Chestnut where he scattered the bottles on the counter in front of the Asian pharmacist. Her almond eyes narrowed with a mixture of pity and apprehension as she filled each prescription. Michael managed to pay with a credit card not yet maxed out. The pharmacist slid the bagged order toward his waxpaper palm, their hands never once touching.

Outside again, Michael found no comfort in the night air as he choked down his pills. Snow thickened on sidewalks and streets. He hobbled home, as graceless as in drunken days. Nearing his corner, he again wished his limbs would unlock what last bit of life they held and let him lay down in the steep snowdrifts beneath the neon blink of the E-Z Lot sign. But a silent message called out to him.

Do not forget me.

He struggled to see its source. Nothing. No one. All the lost boys had yet to climb out of the holes they crawled into.

Blood throbbed beneath Michael's blistering skin. The grim evening was cast in a shadowed blue as cold and complete as air itself.

As Michael neared his door, something in the glow of a street lamp swirled and caught his attention. By the pay phone, air and light cemented into form. First, eyes glinting like glass. Then nose, brow, and chin, their snowy softness packed by rough hands into accidental beauty. Michael, frightened, turned away, crossed the street's shifting drifts, key in hand, its silver point carving a path toward his door.

Behind him, *It's me.*

Could it be? Michael glanced back, turned his key, and let the blue light in the shape of a boy follow him up three flights of stairs to his cramped apartment. There, Michael sat down on his bed, and the boy of light sat down beside him. Moved closer. Blew cool breath over Michael's flushed face as he leaned in to kiss.

Michael woke alone, fever broken. The Blueboy was gone, if indeed he had ever been there.

Michael felt revitalized. Could the medicine really have worked so quickly? Or was it the Blueboy's ghost, whose tongue and mouth had cooled Michael's body? Not with a graveyard chill but with something brought from another world—lifetimes left unused. Lost time conspired into an antidote; Michael could feel it. The Blueboy's ghost an incubus in reverse, a life-giver.

But that was impossible. The Blueboy was obviously still alive, nothing supernatural about it. Someone else must have drowned. Yet Michael could find no evidence that anyone had truly been there the night before; when he rose from bed, his apartment was still locked from inside. The air around him vibrated with the texture of a dream. In the bathroom, he splashed cold water on his face. Despite his body's sudden invigoration, Michael feared his mind had pitched forward into dementia. But when he looked in the bathroom mirror, his eyes looked more lucid than in weeks.

Cleaning up his place, he called Keith, told him he had not gone to Florida after all, but wanted to meet for a walk. Keith enthusiastically agreed to the unexpected invitation.

Hanging up, Michael spied the number he had written on the wall above the nightstand—the corner pay phone. He considered dialing it, but the idea seemed crazy.

When Keith came, they walked uptown, Michael secretly searching for the Blueboy among the winter-wrapped pedestrians. But the young man was not to be found panhandling among shoppers or bumming smokes from office workers on breaks.

As they traipsed down to South Street, Keith complimented Michael's newfound energy. Michael said nothing as he led them along the northern edge of Gray's Ferry. Still no sign of the Blueboy.

Soon they came to the South Street Bridge, where the kid had jumped. Hadn't he? Michael stopped halfway across, ignoring Keith's puzzled expression as he scanned the river winding southward. In the distance behind scraggly trees, refinery smokestacks trailed charcoal wisps. Michael studied the riverside, trying to X-ray with his eyes the abandoned Navy Home in a vain effort to spy the house in Devil's Pocket where the Blueboy had grown up. Where his brother had beaten him. Where he had become convinced life wasn't worth living.

Your spirits are certainly up today, Keith remarked.

Michael snapped around. Behind his companion, the spires of the city rose up—all glass and metallic blue in the afternoon light. The river ran alongside, bright slivers flashing against murky indigo. The colors hurt Michael's eyes. The wind blew sudden cold back into his bones and he found himself shivering.

A few days later, Michael's phone rang in the middle of the night as it had long ago. At first he couldn't believe the faint whisper of the voice in his ear. He crossed to the window and looked down at the street corner. The Blueboy stood by the pay phone, face upturned toward Michael's window.

Soon the boy was at his door. Ushered in, cold and damp, his skin so pale it showed the lace of blue veins beneath.

You're frozen, Michael said, removing both of their clothes. Soon his naked form lay atop the Blueboy's goosebumped skin. Michael tried to warm the Blueboy with hands and mouth. He drew the kid's cock past his lips, glanced up, saw the Blueboy's eyes roll back and shudder in their sockets.

So much coldness to fire, Michael thought. He reached to the nightstand for a condom, started to roll it on when he felt the chill of the Blueboy's hand close around him. *That's not needed anymore*, he said, guiding Michael in.

Inside his chest, Michael felt a silken cord wind tight, the same one that had linked them the night of his fever. Michael let the Blueboy reel him in, rocking against the young man's body, feeling a long-feared part of himself build toward release. Soon his warm come filled the boy's coldness.

Morning came, and Michael awoke alone, door once more locked from inside.

When Keith came to walk Michael to his doctor's appointment, Michael fought the urge to divulge everything, knowing Keith would only roll his eyes. At the hospital, Michael remained moody and silent as the doctor poked and prodded, only the faintest of smiles coloring his lips when he learned his T-cells were up, his physician impressed by his speedy turnaround.

The weather broke. No calls from the Blueboy came. Michael's good health became a trophy Keith showed to his volunteer pals. Michael began to work out with them, meet them for herbal tea, attend their potluck dinners of tofu and tahini. He was glad for company if it meant taking his mind off the Blueboy for awhile. It had been years since he found himself welcomed by a group, though in the back of his mind he thought their chatter rang hollow; their friendship—even Keith's—seemed forced, the charity of the unafflicted.

Still, he gratefully accepted the part-time job Keith arranged for him at the AIDS Fund, where he now spent mornings organizing bingo benefits hosted by drag queens and stuffing envelopes with brochures. Afternoons, Michael climbed the Stairmaster at the gym, sometimes glancing down at his chest, straining to glimpse the silken cord that might at any moment be tugged by an invisible hand. It never was. Evenings, he walked the streets a hustler might haunt, up and down 13th past skinny black drag queens who called out *hey white rooster.* But the Blueboy was never among them, nor inside the bars that Michael checked each night. Spring was in the air and the Blueboy's ghost had been sucked back into the dark.

One afternoon Michael entered St. John's, though he hadn't been to church since his father's funeral. Out of habit he genuflected and crossed himself, then took a seat in back. An old woman crept past to the confessional. When she shut the wooden door, Michael raised his eyes to the vaulted ceiling, its filigreed arches hazy and oiled beneath a veneer of candle soot. Michael sighed and scanned the painted saints. What good would it do to take the old woman's place when she left? The bearded carvings offered no answer. Michael rose, lit a candle before leaving, recalling the distant lights from his dream, how hard it had been to reach them.

And now when night comes, Michael stays up late, dials the number written on the wall above his nightstand. He carries the old black rotary to the window and looks down at the corner where the lost boys gather. Regulars ignore the ringing pay phone as they place their palms on open car windows. Occasionally a curious new boy picks up the pay phone receiver, and Michael listens in silence as a naive *hello* threads through wires to reach his ear.

Fingers point to Michael's window as the newcomer learns who the caller is. A peal of laughter rises. Michael shrinks from the lost boys' sight. He sinks to the floor, hears the pay phone receiver drop and clatter, yanking against its cord. He shuts his eyes, wondering how he can help himself when each upturned face might be the Blueboy's come again—his hand lifting the fallen receiver, his voice whispering *It's me.* Snowflakes fall on the Blueboy's cheeks, collect on his lashes. Michael can feel them melting.

Castro: A Manifesto

Jim Coughenour

Sex line. 10:30 Saturday night. Message just left: "I've got a 29-year-old boy over here who needs to get fucked. Come give him your load. 863-4278." I hang up; hit redial. Busy. Damn! Busy again. Call and listen to the message again, stroking my dick. Hang up. Call. Busy. Call again. Get through. Talk to the Dad. Talk to the boy. Ask where he wants his cum delivered. Mouth. Talk to Dad again. Get his address. Hop in car. Front door's open when I arrive. Dad still on the cell phone, trying to arrange a party. Boy naked on the bed. Strip. Feed him my cock. Start playing with his ass. Fuck him. Dad still on the phone, feeding boy his dick. Come. Go.■

Vowed not to call the lines tonight. I'll never be in a relationship if all I seek is a casual encounter. Call a friend instead. No answer. Leave message. Get a pass code and get undressed. Message #1—done him before. #2—too old. #3—never exactly sure what a "toilet slave" wants. Don't want to go there. #4—same as #1—he must be tweaking. Again. #5—sounds promising so far. Damn, he's a top. #6—too old. #7—the tweaker. #8—the tweaker again. #9—Scott in the Mission, bondage top. #10—that damn cigar chomping Dad. Big bruiser bottom. Gross! #11—tweaker. #12—Lyle at the Leland Hotel on Polk.

Gay sex is contra naturam. That is its horror. That is its joy. ■ Art and Love are necessary only for artists and lovers. Nature needs neither. ■ But we aren't talking about love or art. We're talking about sex. Does nature need gay sex? No. So fuck nature. All culture is combat. (Now we're talking about art and love.) ■ I love the spit-speckled innocence of the moralists who rage against us. Their dogmatic ignorance is our carnal bliss. If only they knew how right they were. What they imagine as exotic perverted rituals we know to be as common as dirt. No sexual practice is too disgusting, shocking, or degrading to be accepted as our

Don't think so. #13—Sounds good: 32, bottom, tall. Get number. Call. He already came, thanks. Fuck. ■

If you're a hungry aggressive masculine guy and you get 90% of your battery charged from a warm wet hole or if your hands are cold, call Mike. Lean and natural, handsome and totally uninhibited. ■

One of my first experiences with the phone sex line was 247-2000. You leave a message and can listen to other messages but it costs $1.98 a minute to retrieve messages—and that's after paying $1.98 a minute to navigate through all the other options to get to the place where you can finally play your messages—and then to waste more time they tell you "message number one" and the time before they actually give you the message. I put out a message saying I was a top and whatever else and had several messages right away. One I called back sounded kind of hot. He was 35 (that was before I knew some people lied on these lines) and he liked getting fucked. After we talked a couple of minutes he asked me if I'd help him with a fantasy of his. He wanted me to come over, his door would be open and his house would be dimly lit. I was to go up the stairs to the first door on the left. He would be sleeping there on his stomach and I could strip down, fuck him, and then leave. It sounded hot so I agreed and got his address. I went over, fucked and left, thinking it was really odd—his letting me in without knowing me. Next time I'll take that great lamp hanging in the entry. ■

Yeah man bottom needs to suck some dick, get fucked man real hard. Give me a call. Lyle. Call me man any time day or night. ■

what are you into *fucking sucking rimming* do you like to fuck or get fucked *get fucked* cool where are you *walnut creek* wow are you coming into the city tonight *i might be are you negative* yeah *wow how can you live in the city and stay negative* it's easy we know how it's transmitted *i just don't think i could do it that's why i moved to walnut creek all my friends were dying* that's a little extreme isn't it when did you move out there *8 years ago i've been slowly dying on the vine for 8 years* why don't you move back to the city *too many bad memories couldn't do it* so i guess that means you're not coming into the city

inalienable right, providing all partners agree. And we eagerly agree to be disgusted, shocked, and degraded. ■ Thus is transgression sanctified, normalized, banalized. Every fetish is a new identity (a new zine, a new bar). This is a mistake. ■ We should always disbelieve our own propaganda. ■ Gay love is the greatest

sin. Fundamentalists cannot comprehend that such love exists: they only comprehend sinful acts. In this misapprehension they are much like gay men. ■ Gay men do have souls, contrary to popular belief, particularly the popular belief of gay men. We twist between spirit and flesh, redeeming one by profaning the other. ■

tonight *no i guess not* do you want my number in case you change your mind or come in over the weekend *no i guess not* ■

TRANSLATION CHART

beard	=	bear
sturdy	=	fat
8 inches	=	6 inches
stocky	=	fat
goatee	=	can't shave
200 lbs	=	fat
work out	=	once
thick	=	average
kinky	=	water sports
raunch	=	scat
party	=	tweaker
toilet slave	=	eek!

this is Scott in the Mission, bondage top looking for bottoms under 35 who are very submissive. you come over I blindfold you. you don't get to see me or the place or what's happening. i strip you down and do whatever i want including fuck your butt. thanks. ■

so how's it going good **what are you into** looking for a bottom who wants me to come over, feed him my dick, get into a mutual rim job, and then have me fuck him **sounds hot I love rimming** cool me too, do you do it well **yeah, I like to get way up in there, have you push it out for me** great **yeah, and then you can push out a turd and make me lick it** -gulp- sounds hot **yeah and then make me eat it. do you want a submissive slave** uh, yeah **I really get into Daddy fantasies** do you have any other fantasies **one night we can meet at Collingwood Park and you can find a dog turd in the lawn and make me get down on my knees and eat it** sounds hot **do you have to take a dump right now** uh, maybe **why don't you go into the bathroom and try. I'd love to hear you dropping a turd.** uh, ok **tell me what you're doing. I want**

Gay "spirituality" is always suspect (what is more repugnant than a gay priest?). We are constitutionally incapable of distinguishing between spirit and flesh—if only because each is the conduit for the other. We don't want to be forgiven our trespasses, we want to hallow them. ■ At the same time, it is essential that sacred

is safeguarded so that there is something to transgress. ■ The only thing we can't forgive is forgiveness. ■ The war between flesh and spirit is won when one man's lips touch another's. ■ Gay men are the victims of obsession—wasting our lives in low places waiting for a connection that never comes. Gay men are the heroes of obsession—converting base need into antic energy. Hence our sparkle. ■ We begin by believing that passion is everything. We conclude by concurring that passion is nothing. Then we begin again. ■ Death is incidental. Tragedy is denied, repressed, and decorated. AIDS is merely an excuse for a circuit party.

to hear it all. well, I'm sitting down on the toilet **yeah, sounds hot** and I'm pushing **oooh, yeah** and I can feel something coming out **oh yeah... is it soft or hard?** hard. **oh yeah! what else?** well, it's coming out *-plop-* **OH YEAH! OH YEAH! dude, that was so hot! I want you to save it for me and make me bob it out of the toilet tonight** ok **what's your number** why don't I call you? I share this phone **ok, it's 771-8245** great, I'll call you tonight **sounds hot. save me that turd.** ok—*click —flush* ■

Things you will need to start connecting with people on the lines: Paper. Pencil. A height/weight proportionate chart. And a description of yourself that you will repeat over and over again until it bears only a tangential resemblance to whoever you once imagined yourself to be. ■

One Saturday night in the back of Badlands I see this lanky blond guy, says he's a screenwriter from LA. Surprise. We have a couple beers, the bar closes, I don't want to take him home because I just washed the sheets. Where to go? Well, I think, there's End Up. We cab it, pay the cover, and find a dark sofa back by the fireplace. It takes us maybe 45 minutes to realize that the crowd is black, the music reggae, and that people are doing their best to ignore our orgy in the corner. We retract our tongues and start thinking options. Well, there's Blow Buddies. What's that? A sex club right around the corner. OK. We get new memberships, check our shirts and walk back by the piss area. I start running my hands down his chest and he immediately goes limp, sagging against the cum-stained wall like a raggedy Andy. Oh great. I turn him around and smack his ass. He moans. I jerk his pants down and smack it again, hard. He moans. Harder. We do this for a minute or two then he leans back and whispers *Now you know I can take it.* Fine. I go back to the front and check out a rubber paddle. I go back and pull his shorts down around his knees and let him have it. He's in heaven. I hear something behind me and this big flannel daddy is nodding and growling and grabbing his crotch. Here, I said, handing him the paddle. You're into this. I'm not. ■

■ Safe sex is not hot sex. Hot sex is lethal. For gay men this counts as a moral dilemma. ■ Gay men are essentially playful. ■ Sometimes it's very hard to like gay men. Unless they're in drag (Nothing is more delightful than a penis in a dress). ■ No one is more tedious than a "straight-acting gay." No one is more fun to rape. ■ Gay men are cartoons. For gay men pornography is a reality principle. ■ Porn stars—who at certain furtive moments represent the unattainable acme of gay actualization—are as disposable as dreams. They are the waste of fantasy. Rarely has worship been so reduced: to something shot in the hand

Later LA finds me again, back in that dark stinky enclosure with the barber chair. I'm weary. I just don't have the energy to play Master tonight. Look, I tell him, climb on that stool over there, pull your pants down, and stand there until someone sucks your dick. He obeys. I leave him there and find someone to blow me. ■

A letter arrives from Pacific Bell: You've spent over $75 this month on 900 calls. We can reverse the charges one time if this is an error. I think: only $75? I remember when all I used to waste was time. ■

One night I picked up this guy in Collingwood Park and went over to his house. He was a street punk, sexy in a grungy beware-of-crabs kind of way. We had a pretty good time, though he wouldn't let me fuck him and I felt faintly ridiculous kneeling over him so I could come on his chest as he kept begging me to do. After he'd rubbed my cum into his pelt of chest hair, he asked me if I liked wolves.—?—Sure, I said. He said he loved them—in fact he'd once been a wolf and felt lost being human. I stretched for empathy, but it was difficult, standing there naked in my socks and sweaty T-shirt with my cock hanging out. Wolfboy starts making these tormented tiny whimpering noises. Next he was on all fours nuzzling against my leg. Cowering at my feet, being very submissive—which never excites me the way people expect it to. He gives my calf a wet, tentative lick. *Okay*...I bend over to pet him, scratch him a little behind the ears. He barks. I leave. ■

I'm in Detour trying to piss in the back trough, my eyes closed. I'm trying to imagine that I'm alone. I feel someone grab my dick. "Hey man give me some of that." I open my eyes and stare at the pierced shaved head staring at me. "Sorry, dude," I say, "but I don't have sex in toilets. I need it to mean something more." n

Oh God, it's 3:00 already and I promised myself I wouldn't be out cruising Collingwood Park past 2:30. Oh well...I'll go home by 4. No, I'll be ***in bed*** *by 4. I can get four hours of sleep before work.—Okay, since I have an hour, I'll drive over to the peep shows on Folsom. Maybe there'll be someone there who's interesting. But that's 10 minutes there and 10 minutes*

or wiped off the sheet—out of testes, out of mind. ■ Gay men's taste is wildly overrated. If it weren't for the appalling aesthetics of most gay men (rainbow trinkets, Billy dolls, penis pasta) the Castro would go bankrupt. ■ However, gay wit is deservedly celebrated. Ask anyone who's ever endured a gay office temp.

back. Maybe I should try the Black House. Except for the skanky street-punks who hang out in the kitchen and dish everybody walking by, it isn't so bad. But that's $8.00. Maybe I should go to Buena Vista park... ■

Some nights I just can't bring myself to call the line. It's too depressing to hear the same people night after night, parroting the same monotonous needs in the same desperately bored voices—Mike, Lyle at the Leland, that gross cigar-chomping daddy. It's just like the peep shows or the Black House. Each place has its tired group of regulars that you pick your way through, then humiliate yourself by seeing them again and again. Years ago when I used to go to the baths, there was this hairy ogre who'd pad after me in his towel, shadowing me from sauna to steam room to orgy room and back again. No matter what night I'd go, he'd show up, never getting the message that I considered him repulsive. Last Christmas I went home for a visit and stopped by the baths—and there he was, older and uglier than ever. He caught my scent and was on the trail again. Nothing changes. ■

Yeah, this raunch pig is looking for a feeding tonight. I want a big fat juicy turd sliding down my throat. If you're 44 or younger, attractive and in good shape like I am, and you're interested in feeding tonight, page me. Willing to stay in or travel. ■

I don't get this scat thing. ■

Why do I not want to write about Chris? Because he's special? Because he might be The One? He's so cute, and young and *we have similar backgrounds.* He was so shy the afternoon he came over. I liked him from the start; I liked him a lot. He knew what he wanted and was embarrassed by his desire. He was tall and smooth and I loved the way he tossed his hair back. He was eager to kiss, and touch, and got undressed as quickly as he could. He told me he wanted to get fucked and because he was nervous, we got right to it. I had him on his back and started licking his tight young butt. Then I greased up and began fucking him. It took awhile to get all the way in but he was obviously enjoying it. I loved having him on his back under me where I watch the feeling in his face, the way he'd clench

Gay office temps are glitter of corporate culture—perhaps the only quality that redeems the toll they take on copying machines. ■ Gay men enact their mothers' id. We triumphantly resolve the Oedipus complex at our parents' expense. ■ The most radical act a gay man can perform is to refuse to be radically gay. ■ Identity politics liberated gay men, but gay men will never be free until identity politics disappear. This will never happen because gay men are instinctually despised. ■ Most gay fiction is propaganda. Some of it is useful to teenagers. ■ Teenagers should steer clear of Dennis Cooper. ■ Larry Kramer and Edmund White are each wrong. Together they tell truth—but only when they contradict each other. ■ In the grammar of gay men, love is stated in the past imperfect, lust in the present indicative, sex in the imperative. Gay grammar has no future tense, only an optative mood. ■ Gay sex is regressive, gay love transcendental. Gay men only create

his teeth and shut his eyes every time I pushed a little deeper. God, he was great. I loved kissing him while my dick was inside him. I could do that all day, just moving in and out of him, watching his face. Having him tell me how much he loved it, telling me I could fuck him anytime I wanted, that his ass belonged to me. We really developed a rhythm, a synergy that afternoon—the breeze coming through the room. He shot all over his chest, then I pulled out and came on him. It wasn't like the usual routine where I steer the guys around so they don't shoot where I plan to sleep, when their spermy puddles gross me out. We rested together and kept giggling, the way it sometimes happens after really intense sex. I could sense myself falling for him. We showered together, washing each other's chests, arms, butts, cocks. I watched him dry off and got another boner. We tossed around on the bed some more but didn't ejaculate. Watching him get dressed was like finishing a favorite book. He gave me his number. He already had mine from the lines. As he was leaving I rubbed his shoulder and he seemed surprised that I was still affectionate. Didn't he realize how much he got me going? How much I wanted to start all over? I wanted back inside. ■

I called him immediately after he left to say thanks, but it was his work number. Why did he give me his work number? Does he have a boyfriend? Is that why he seemed so nervous? Damn. He was so perfect. I got back in the shower again, and replayed the whole afternoon in my mind. I wanted to remember everything. Our conversation on the line, his anxious laugh at my jokes, the way he described himself—and first seeing him at my door. The taste of his ass. It's been almost 3 weeks and he hasn't called. Maybe he's on vacation? I just want to run my fingers through his hair. I get hard thinking about kissing him. His sweet face. ■

I guess I expected that I'd hear from him by now. I don't want to jinx this one. I want to stay upbeat. I wonder if he'll call. Some nights after I've been on the lines for a few hours, I call his number at work. I know he won't be there. I just want to hear his voice.

to the extent that they are deprived of animal expression. Culture is the child of lust and melancholy. ■ Gay consciousness is the matrix of the next stage of human evolution. This should give us pause. ■ Gay is always an adjective, never a noun.

Six Positions

Andy Quan

I'm making love to the oldest man I've ever been with. His hair is white as Egyptian silk, his skin is translucent, blue and pink. I can see his heart beating from excitement. I am drawing an arrow down with my tongue, shoulder to opposite hip, a ribbon of saliva like a banner from a beauty pageant. This one says, "This man has tasted and been tasted by men for decades." Blood ricochets around his body and builds at his surprising erection. The wrinkles on his face, arms, hands, so loose, a multitude of scrotums all over his body, which I take into my mouth like dinosaur eggs, rare plums, a tulip's head unopened. With veneration, I lift, squeeze softly, hear a gasp like an ocean caught in shells. It is the last ocean. It is wet. The tide recedes like sadness.

I'm making love to the fattest man I've ever been with. His anus cannot be found amidst the mounds of flesh, but his mouth, pink, red, puckering, surrounded by two round cheeks, has a passing resemblance. He laughs a great thrusting belly laugh for the whole time we grapple, him turning and flopping, me dodging the weight whirling all around for my own safety. Every part of my body is a phallus, my fingers, hands, arms, legs, head. I press these into skin that says, yes! and takes me in, out, in, out, sweating, sliding, surrounded by warmth, by darkness. Somewhere in this maze I find a cock that is fat and round like a root vegetable. I punch at it, grasp it with my hungry hands, hear a voice as if outside of a room or all around, of god, of a pregnant mother, *huh huh huh*. The sticky fat flood smells of appetite.

I'm making love to the most exotic man I've ever been with. He has eyes like jungle animals. Tigers, wildebeests, possums, crocodiles, sloths, night owls. His skin turns color depending on the angle of light: dark as petroleum, as the center of your skull, then yellow as the eyes of those jungle animals. As slight as a bamboo reed, then a tight round muscularity on fire with bound-up strength. Then two-breasted and big-cocked and more pictures, pretty pictures, so many I'm almost blind and I fuck him I fuck him I fuck him until I am covered in the fluids of my own exertion, thigh muscles, stomach, arms, still tensed, energy hanging on me still. Shivering, and when the thought returns to my head, I understand him not a bit more.

I'm making love to the thinnest man I've ever been with. He is so thin and long that he is sharp. I bleed with pleasure. He presses his fingers down on me and leaves a lovely symmetrical arc, five small half-moon-shaped pricks. The air on my skin, and my cuts, feels spiny like a cactus, a tall spindly one with a downy white veil of spikes. Like pins and needles, when a part of your body has fallen asleep, and you have to shake and shake to get the blood back in. I am in a desert of sensation, so quiet that every grain of sand is noticeable. But I do not notice as he clothes himself head to foot in rubber and enters me from behind. I don't know if it's his penis, his arm, his leg, his whole body. I just remember he's thin. It's suddenly an Arizona night and the stars are twinkling in time with an orgasm soon to arrive. Sensation pours through the star-holes, the rest is black. Each time I exhale, one of the stars goes out.

I'm making love to the smallest man I've ever been with. Small is beautiful. He has attached his mouth to my cock, his legs dangling down. I feel *enormous*, I am enormous in comparison. He leaps and lands on my tit, and bounces on my nipple as if it were a trampoline, does cartwheels and somersaults up my stomach, around my neck. My touch on him is crude but large; he rubs into it like a cat, then returns to my crotch where he gives special attention to each square millimeter. When he finishes the last, I explode. I worry I've drowned him, but he shakes himself off in a triumphant dance, slides down my leg and disappears.

I'm making love to myself. Really. With elasticity and extra parts, I am seeing what all the others have seen before me, I am tasting my nipples, which come alive and harden, punctuation marks in the air all around me. My voice, *oh oh oh*—periods. *Uh uh uh*—commas. *Awuhaaahh*—question mark. Gasping hyphens, sighing slants, I grunt out underlines. I am writing myself onto my page as my cock extends long, so long, I'm entered. I'm thrusting into myself. I have ten hands. I have eight tongues. A line between my balls and thigh. The slit in my throbbing head. A dimple where chest meets abdominals. All fingered. All stroked. All tongued. The skin of the page curves into its wet stain. Words run into each other.

Million-to-One Shot

horehound stillpoint

Muscles leaned against walls. Hard, high pecs swaggered by. Jam-packed buns disappeared around corners.

No doubt about it: there was some real pretty shit, out and about, this Saturday night in the city.

I was feeling just the teeniest bit crazy. I mean, men everywhere, half nude, pumped, everything up for grabs, and nothing much going on. One of those nights when you can't help thinking, shit, fifty billion galaxies evolved over fifteen billion years across immeasurable reaches of space so that we could end up hauling our oversexed asses through this maze of desire yet again.

Doors to tiny booths banged open and closed. Two hundred different faces of intense masculinity shifted, flowed, grouped, groped, and scattered. The shooting gallery of glory holes, though full to bursting, lacked energy.

Hungry ghosts.

Unblinking eyes, set on scan. Chiseled smooth cheekbones. Hardline jaws. Bluejeans and biceps. Leather jocks, bulging Calvins, and cut-off sweats, hanging low. Everyone glistened.

Sweaty business, this running the labyrinth of our lust.

Johnny Cash sang about his ring of fire and how it burned…sampled, over a techno beat.

On the video, a man with his head in a black leather hood demonstrated an impressive array of sex tools on an all-American boy-next-door. A moment of relief, just to watch. Do me, TV.

This sex club palace of cocksucking pleasure cum torture cum addiction cum surrender cum release cum disease cum ecstasy feels too deeply queer for words, some nights. And one of these nights, it might be the death of me.

One decision left: to leave…or…to dive in, and give it everything I've got.

Dive.

One hungry ghost—all tongue and pawing desperation—lunged at me. He exuded the breath of a man who's already had seven greasy honkers in his mouth. His body generated an entire cloud of odors: licked armpits, sucked asses, cheap beer, swilled piss, and cum. Plenty of cum.

On the right night, that could taste pretty good. If you were in the mood.

Everything depended on how many inches of desire you were packing, how many quarts of boy-juice you were willing to share, and how much old baggage could be dropped off outside the door. Sometimes it seemed like more trouble than it was worth, squeezing out a tablespoon of joy, in a fucked up world like this.

Until the right man comes along.

Turn a corner, and everything changes.

Cause there he was.

Walking with a balls-out biker's attitude, with a nice, sleazy smile in his eyes, this dude, this man, arrived like fresh air. He wore nothing but funky, dirty work boots and a tattoo that read BOYD over his left nipple,

He looked like he was strictly from Detroit.

Heads turned.

His big ol' meat swinging, Boyd walked with a cockiness that came from knowing everything there was to know about his place in the universe. At five years old, he'd had a dream, remembering what it was like in his mother's womb. Safe. Warm. Wet. Silent, and utterly blissful. Later dreams revealed to him his previous lives, and the incredibly repetitive nature of birth, and death…birth and death. The last dream in this series showed him the entire string of causality that had led to All This, the whole world in which every twig, every brick, every star, and every spark plug made perfect sense. Boyd knew what he was. He knew he was born to be a great mechanic, take care of his invalid mother, and fuck as many men as he could in the brief amount of time this body would last.

Tonight, as every night, he was on a mission from God.

I followed him into the back room. I was not alone.

Boyd went right over to a black guy wearing a leather harness and chaps, and said:

"Hey, partner, what's your name?"

"Benny," answered the guy, with a friendly but guarded half-sneer.

"Well, I'm Boyd, and I don't believe in anonymous sex, so I sure am glad you tol' me yer name."

Then Boyd kissed Benny so pure and so rough that all of us watching hoisted hard-ons in about ten seconds. Kept on kissing too, as Boyd started pulling on Benny's dark, uncut dick. Pumping it and rubbing it on his belly, between his thighs, working up sweat and precum and saliva that flowed with the kiss that would not stop, would not let go. It looked like Benny was getting a blow job from the top down, turning every inch of his skin, every ounce of his blood and every bone of his skeleton into a single sex organ. He started thrashing and writhing as if he had the fullest, hottest load since Krakatoa.

Benny's first cum shot blasted so high, it caught them both under the chin, and Benny jerked, but Boyd kept that kiss full on, pedal to the metal and to hell with going over a cliff. The jism squirted up Boyd's chest, covered his tattoo, and mushed into his nipples before oozing into his hairy belly and mixing with the sweat dripping off his heavy hanging balls.

Boyd used one of Benny's hands to spread semen over any areas that got missed. Then he pushed his tongue into this big, beautiful, butch, black man who appeared to be experiencing some mysterious melting shudder in his core. He was finished.

With that, Boyd let the kiss dissolve.

"Stick around," he whispered into Benny's ear. As if Benny were going anywhere.

Boyd looked right at me. I wasn't ready for that spotlight yet, but there it was. He came straight over and licked my ear with a tongue that slobbered over the entire side of my head, just like a big old dog.

"What's yer name, little stud?"

"Greg."

"Talk ta me, Greg. Tell me whatcha want."

"Uhhhh…"

I don't know why I was shaking so hard, why I lost my cool and my voice all at once.

"Whisper it in mah ear."

If I had been anywhere near my body, I would have told myself to breathe.

Then that slow devilish smile crept across Boyd's face.

"I betcha I know what you want, anyhow."

But God the Father had handed me some urges difficult to name. I wanted to be his baby, his one and only son. I wanted to be brought down to my psychic knees and do something wrong and weird and unusual. In the calculus of lust, anything can equal bliss. In the algebra of fulfillment, God is as blank and ever-present as the x-factor.

Not terribly helpful.

But Boyd's smile did help. For a moment, it convinced me that this was just between the two of us, and the rest of the universe could go fuck itself into absolute zero.

So, quietly, in his ear, I told him what I wanted.

"Bee-yuu-ti-ful," Boyd replied. "Tell ya what, Greg; I'm gonna make all yer dreams come true. Jus' not yet. I'm gonna save you fer later. Don't go far, though," he said, licking me some more, my chin, my eyes, my neck. "Don't go anywhere."

Boyd worked the whole room with the same precision, the same grace, the same dirt-loving masculinity that made him such an asset in the garage.

An Asian guy, with a chiseled chest, a twenty-seven inch waist, and a genuine bubble butt, smiled at Boyd with a dick-licking grin. His name was Junior. The mechanic surprised everyone by squatting in a corner, and looking up at Junior with a fierce purpose in his eyes. Whacking his meat with one hand, Boyd stuck a big ol' finger up Junior's asshole and pushed about thirty-seven buttons in no time, slick as shit. The finger was then pulled out, one knobby knuckle at a time, while the two men stared each other down. Slowly, Boyd brought his finger around to his face, sniffed it, licked it, and rolled it around in his mouth like a favorite-flavor lollipop. Another finger went in, and Junior said to himself, in his last conscious thought:

"This guy is really gonna clean my clock."

Eight fingers and two thumbs later, Junior felt the hot rush that meant he was gonna shoot. The mechanic's rough red lips were busy, and that big ol' tongue was curled up into the shape of a saucer. The message was clear:

"Lay your load right here, young pup."

At the last minute, Junior opened his eyes and watched as he popped his nuts in the big man's face. Once all the splooge had found its mark, Boyd whapped his tongue and sent that jism flying into the back of his throat and down his gullet. He grinned—

such a grin—the "cocksucker who's just gotten the cream" kind of grin.

"Thanks, Junior."

"Mmmph," the little guy whimpered.

"Know what?" the mechanic remarked, before they parted. "We're inside each other now, fer good."

The night continued.

Jason, the burly white dude who looked like a wrestler gone to seed, got the full *who's a top* and *who's a bottom* treatment.

Manuel, the smooth Latin loverboy with one eye permanently half-closed, got a sensuous, silken, feather-light touch lavished upon his flesh, from his big toe to his inner ear. When he came—and he came a buttload—time collapsed in on itself and the walls shuddered and everyone in the back room (even guys who were otherwise engaged) looked up, like animals in a forest who feel the first rumble, the little shock, which may or may not indicate a big ol' quake to come.

Kip, the downy blonde beach bum, got the grungy mechanic's shop talk: "Get those pistons pumping, buddy. We're gonna change your oil right now, lube you up, strip you down. Do you a major overhaul, yeah. Pull those spark plugs, and tune you right up. Give you the wax job you deserve. Wheeyuuew, yer boilin' over. Time to tweak those nuts and blow those bolts, buddy. Come on Kip, gun it, baby, rev it up and let it go. Let's see what yer engine's made of."

With their hands on the wall, the surfer dude has his blonde dick sliding all over the mechanic's crack. The testosterone level of the grease-monkey poetry made Kip squirt about a quart of his own, all over Boyd's knotty muscled butt.

The mechanic was nothing if not versatile. He knew from service.

It was easy to get lost in the performance.

Easy to lust from a distance.

When Boyd worked his way back to me, and planted that

unadulterated kiss into my mouth, I felt as if I were being pulled down into a relentless and irresistible whirlpool. My brain turned to mush. My skin turned to cream. My tongue got a boner. My blood flowed into another man's heart.

Dangerous territory.

Boyd grabbed my ass and lifted me off the ground. I felt his cock between my legs, and it held me up like a pole. With my back against the wall, my cock dipped in the sweat of the mechanic's belly, and I thought I would die.

I could feel his balls slapping against my thighs.

"You wanna get married, backroom style? You got it, buddy."

He kissed me again, and then became still. Energy shifted; something dropped, something let go. He spoke into my mouth, so that both our lips formed the words.

"I take you, in front of God an' everybody. W'thout fear, w'thout shame. I do, Greg, I do."

And suddenly—whoooooshh—the steaming wet surge of the mechanic's piss spilled out over my butt and down my legs. Liquid love.

I had wanted it so bad, for so long. That river of gold might as well have been tears of joy. No matter what anyone says, it is a holy moment, when you get your heart's desire. A whole life can seem to make sense, anew.

But instead of tears, I unleashed my own hot stream onto Boyd's rippled belly. Our skin was awash in piss, our noses filled up with heavy smells, and the temperature of the jism in our balls rose another ten degrees.

Things quickly got wetter and more slippery, and I started to fall. Boyd pulled us away from the concrete wall; we tumbled to the floor and rolled in all the cum that all the men had spilled and all the piss that was flying around the room, and still we kissed. Stroking and pulling our dicks and pissing in each other's faces and in our hair, the shower of gold reached the boiling point.

We shot like cannons.

We shot while we were still pissing.

We pissed the walls into the void and then splashed the void to smithereens.

Everybody came with us. Everybody came, pure and simple. No holding back. No saving anything for later. The whole room went orgasmic. And beyond. The mechanic entered into a field of awareness without limits, and he brought us along for the ride.

Bodies got left behind. Names were utterly forgotten. Nothing could be seen. No one was left to see. Nothing needed to be done. Pure being. Pure bliss. Eternal, shining bliss.

The substratum of the universe.

Everything else dissolved.

Awareness alone remained. Blissful. Empty. Unborn.

The mechanic tuned us all up.

It lasted forever.

Then, the world came back—an infinitely complex puzzle. It reassembled itself, simultaneously, with the first thought. The void returned and covered awareness like a veil of ignorance, and there was the abyss, the primal cause of so much fear. Over this veil came light and shadow, joy and sorrow, all the dualities, the pairs of opposites, gain and loss.

So much loss.

The non-dual vision: gone.

The infinite, ever-present bliss: covered up.

The boundless sense of awareness: already a memory.

Love, however, remained.

In his eyes, there was love. A sense of belonging, and knowing home. Finding something nameless and beautiful in each other. No dream was ever better.

When everything dissolved, love remained. Then a wonderful,

peaceful silence settled in and lasted for a long, long time.

Boyd suddenly looked at his watch. It was time to get back home and check on his bedridden mother. Without so much as a by-your-leave or a single, scribbled phone number, he left.

Disappeared.

Leaving the rest of us to wonder what had taken place in the dark recesses of our minds, in the wee hours of the night. We could hardly look at each other. We wandered away, got dressed, went back out into the world. Wondering if anything had really happened inside those walls…anything at all.

I thought, for a second, I could taste the bliss again. That cum-drenched warehouse made everything seem so unreal. I wondered if Boyd was who we thought he was or if we would remember him in six months. I hoped, as I staggered down the street, that something of him would linger inside me.

Turning a corner, I couldn't help smiling, as I whispered to myself:

Boyd.

Real or not, my Lord…you sure were a big ol' thing.

Stavros' Place

Bob Vickery

The alley is shabby, but the door at the end of it isn't. It can't be seen from the street; the alley takes two twists before finally ending in a crumbling, stucco wall in which the door is set. But now, standing in front of it, I notice its darkly gleaming wood, the heavy brass knocker, recently polished, set below a peephole. Next to it, screwed into the wall, is an equally well-polished brass plate with the single word: Stavros. I grasp the knocker and rap loudly.

For a long time nothing happens. I wonder if the place is empty. In the distance I hear a baby crying, and I think of young Dimitri. The peephole suddenly slides open and a bloodshot blue eye peers out at me. "What do you want?" a gruff voice asks.

I take my cap off and hold it in both my hands. "Please, I would like to see Mr. Stavros."

The eye rolls down, taking in my patched shirt, my trousers stained with dried fish blood. "What for?"

I keep my gaze level with the eye fixed on my face. "I am looking for work," I say.

There's a bark of laughter from the other side of the door. "Go away," the voice says. The peephole slams shut.

I stand for a minute, staring at the door. Then I turn slowly and start walking down the alley. I hear the door suddenly open behind me. "Hey, you!" the voice calls after me. I turn back to see an old man with the face of a hyena standing in the doorway. "Come in," he says. "Mr. Stavros might be interested in seeing you, after all."

I follow the old man into a small hallway with whitewashed walls. There's a fountain at the end of it, and a straight-backed, wooden chair. The old man nods at it. "Sit there." He disappears behind another door. I wait a long time, staring at the fountain. In its center stands a statue of a young girl, holding a tipped vase. A steady stream of water pours out of the vase into the pool. I close my eyes, the music of the tinkling water filling my ears.

The old man opens the door again. "Mr. Stavros will give you five minutes," he says. He walks away, not bothering to see if I'm following. I jump to my feet and scurry after him, down a dark hallway lit by narrow windows that run just beneath the ceiling. It is late afternoon, and the sun's rays slant in, laced with dust motes. The old man takes me to a closed door. He knocks, opens it, and walks away without a word.

I stand in the open doorway. The room is small but has the feel of luxury to it. A Turkish rug, pale blue and rose, lies on the floor before a wide desk, as polished and richly grained as the door outside. A ceiling fan whirs softly overhead. A man, Stavros presumably, sits behind the desk in a leather upholstered chair. He is the fattest man I have ever seen. He regards me with half-lidded eyes, set like raisins in the thick pudding of his face. "Petros tells me you are looking for work," he says, his voice soft and tired.

"Yes, sir," I say.

"Do you know what kind of establishment this is?" Stavros' eyes are sleepy, bored.

"Yes." I pause. "This is a place where men...pleasure other men."

Stavros regards me silently for a very long time. Fat spills out from under his shirt collar, giving the impression that his head is melting in thick, uneven lumps. I shift my weight to my other foot. "What is your name?" he finally asks.

"Nikos Kazanzakis."

"How old are you, Nikos?"

"Twenty, sir."

Stavros sighs. "Have you ever 'pleasured' a man before? Do you even understand what such a term means?"

"I am a quick learner, " I say, choosing my words carefully. "And I'm good with my hands." This was not meant as a joke, but Stavros' mouth curves up into a thin smile.

He leans forward. "Why do you want to work here?"

"I'm a fisherman," I say. "From the island of Hydros. I have a wife and an infant son, who depend on me for their survival." I try to keep my voice even, but the mention of Kyria and Dimitri is like a knife in my heart. "The fishing season has been poor this year. The waters are fished out, empty of life. I've come to Athens looking for work." I wipe my hand across my forehead. In spite of the fan, the air in the room hangs heavy with heat.

"But I have not been able to find any. In a park in the Plaka district I heard about this place. Men were talking about it." I look Stavros full in the face. "And so I thought I would look for work here."

Stavros gives a low, rumbling laugh that makes his jowls tremble. "This is a well-appointed establishment," he says. "My clients include many rich and powerful men. Do you think I would hire any bumpkin, out-of-work fisherman that knocks on my door?"

I feel the blood rush to my face. I wait until I can trust myself to answer without insult. "No, sir," I say. "Forgive me. I was foolish to come here." I turn to go.

"Stand still!" Stavros barks. I stop. His eyes scan my body. "Come back tomorrow at eleven o'clock."

I feel a surge of hope. "Does this mean…"

"This interview is over." Stavros dismisses me with a wave of his hand. "Good day."

This time, when I knock, Petros lets me in right away. "Follow me," he says. His tone is curt, but at least he no longer talks to me as if I were some stray mongrel. He leads me down a different hall; one side opens into a courtyard, the walls dazzling white in the late morning sun. Potted flowers ring another fountain, this one a trio of stone dolphins with water spouting out of their mouths. A breeze bends the arc of the water, and a light mist brushes my face. Petros knocks on a door and barks, "He's here."

The door opens. A young man stands in the doorway, dressed in a thin silk robe. His skin is dark and his hair is deep black, which make the blue of his eyes all the more startling. I have never seen eyes that shade before, the turquoise of the sea in shallow water. His robe is the same color, and flows across his body like a cascading stream. He smiles, and his teeth gleam in his dark face. "Come in, Nikos," he says. "I apologize for Petros. He has the manners of a goat."

I walk into a dim room, the blinds of the window drawn so that only thin beams of sunlight filter in. There's a bed at the far end, a couple of chairs, a side table with a pitcher and basin, a small rug, nothing more. "I thought I was going to see Mr. Stavros," I say.

The young man shakes his head. "I am Mr. Stavros'…agent. He has asked me to conduct this interview." He smiles his brilliant smile again. "My name is Gregor." His eyes flicker from my face down my body then back to my face. "Mr. Stavros was right. You're very handsome."

"Mr. Stavros said that?"

"No, not in so many words. But you wouldn't have been called back for a second interview if he didn't think that." Gregor settles himself into a chair. "Please remove your clothes."

"Wh…what?"

Gregor smiles. "Nikos, forgive me, but in this establishment, modesty is not a virtue. Your coin of entrance here is your beauty. I must determine the value of that coin before we can consider your employment." He gestures. "Please."

I hesitate, then pull off my shirt and my shoes. I undo the top three buttons of my trousers, then freeze.

"If you don't wish to do this, Nikos," Gregor says softly, "we can always end the interview now."

"No," I say quickly. "I'm fine." I pull down my trousers and kick them aside. I stand naked in front of Gregor.

Gregor's gaze slides slowly down my body, then back up. "Turn around, please," he says.

I turn. Even with my back to Gregor, I can feel the warmth of his gaze. I stop when I'm facing him again. Gregor's eyes gleam. "You really are quite beautiful, Nikos," he says softly. He reaches over and traces his fingers down the side of my face. "I love your eyes, they're so dark and liquid. There's a shyness in them, but underneath the shyness, a fierceness. I can see that you could be a dangerous man if roused to anger." His fingers rest lightly on my lips. "Your mouth is beautifully formed, the lips very full and sensual. It would be a great pleasure to kiss such a mouth." His hand slides down my torso. "And your body…" Gregor shakes his head. "Nikos, your body is magnificent. Fishing must be hard work, for you to have such powerful muscles. And yet there's a grace to your body that I find heartbreaking." His hand slides behind me, running down my back. He squeezes my ass cheeks. "I have not seen such an ass as yours except in museums, carved in marble on statues of gods, Apollo maybe, or Dionysus." He wraps his other hand around my cock. "And your prick! Nikos, your prick is a work of art: thick, fleshy, veined." He strokes it. "It must take one's breath away, when hard."

Gregor smiles and steps back. "Nikos, you are blushing."

My face warms fiercely. "No man has said such things to me. Or touched me in that way."

Gregor leans back in his chair, his smile still on his lips. "Does it displease you?"

"No, " I say carefully. "I don't find your behavior displeasing." I pause. "Just…strange."

Gregor laughs. "Well, get used to it, Nikos. Because if you work here, you will get this from the clients regularly." Gregor stands up and undoes the sash of his robe. With a shrug of his shoulders, the robe falls to his feet. He stands in front of me, naked. "All right, Nikos," he says, "Now I must see how skilled you are in pleasuring a man. I want you to suck my cock." His voice is calm and level, as if this conversation between us were perfectly ordinary. His cock is already half erect; it presses against his thigh, brown and meaty, the head like a dark, round pebble.

My head swims with confusion. "Gregor," I protest. "You go too fast."

Gregor's expression is sympathetic. "Forgive me, Nikos. But I must see how deep your commitment is. If you find this kind of work…distasteful, then it is better I discover, rather than some client." He looks at me expectantly.

I drop to my knees. His dick is fully hard now, throbbing, inches from my face. I grasp it with my hand and squeeze it. I have never touched another man's prick, and the air hums with unreality. I lean forward and slide my mouth down the shaft. I bob my head back and forth, my eyes shut tight.

After a minute Gregor pulls back, freeing his dick from my mouth. "Nikos," he says gently. "You are very clumsy at this." I feel the blood rush to my face again, but I say nothing. "Do you even know what a good blow job feels like?"

I don't answer immediately. "My wife," I say slowly, "is a virtuous and modest woman."

"Ah," Gregor says, nodding. "I understand." He laughs.

"Fortunately I am neither virtuous nor modest. So perhaps I can give you some useful instruction. Stand up."

I climb to my feet, and Gregor drops to his knees before me. He cradles my dick in the palm of his hand and looks up at me. "Sucking dick is a subtle art," he says. "You must lead up to it slowly, tease the client." The gentle cradle becomes a strong squeeze. "Pay close attention, Nikos. First, I will start with your balls." He buries his nose in my balls and breathes deeply. His tongue flicks across the sac, first lightly and then with increasing force. He opens his mouth and my balls spill inside. He sucks on them, rolls them with his tongue, his eyes never leaving mine. Tingles of pleasure shoot through my body. Still sucking on my nut sac, he slides his hands up my torso and grips my nipples. He squeezes them, hard. I groan, and my dick swells to full stiffness, laying heavily against his cheek.

Gregor slowly slides his tongue up the shaft of my dick. When he gets to the head, he swirls his tongue around it, probing into my piss slit. He presses his lips against the head and leaves them there for a moment. I'm breathing heavily now. He looks at me, his eyes playful. "Notice how that makes you hungry for more, Nikos," he says. "How much you wish me to suck on your dick now. Sometimes it's good to torment the client, make him wait. The moment of gratification is all the sweeter." Without warning, he slides his lips full down my shaft. His mouth moves up and down my dick, drawing out sensations that flood over me like warm sea water. He stops and again looks up at me.

"Are you paying attention, Nikos?" he asks. "You mustn't lose yourself in the sensations. You must learn these techniques."

I open my eyes. "Yes, Gregor," I say. "I'm paying attention."

Gregor continues sucking my cock. Once more, pleasure washes over me, and it is with the greatest difficulty that I keep from sinking into it. Gregor removes his mouth from my cock. "Did you see how I twisted my head from side to side as I sucked? This increases the sensations along the shaft. And how I rolled my tongue around your dick? And yes, I do suck, it's not just a figure of speech. I seal my lips tight around your dick and create a partial vacuum in my mouth. This creates sensations of great pleasure for a man."

"I understand," I say. A rivulet of sweat trickles down my forehead, and I wipe it quickly with the back of my arm.

Gregor reaches beside the chair and picks up a small green bottle. He pours several drops of thick white liquid into his hand. He rubs the cream over his fingers. "Spread your legs farther apart," he says.

I obey. Gregor reaches under my legs, and his hand pries apart my ass cheeks. His fingers burrow inside the crack and massage my asshole. One finger pushes inside me. I instinctively clamp my ass muscles tight.

"Relax, Nikos," he says. "Accept what I'm doing to you." I try to obey, willing my ass muscles to relax. Gregor's finger pushes in deeper, as he returns to sucking my cock. This time his other hand is wrapped around my dick, following his lips as they slide up and down the shaft, his finger fucking my ass in long, slow thrusts. I groan loudly, and my knees tremble.

Gregor pulls away, amused. "I think you are beginning to learn how much pleasure a man's body is capable of, Nikos," he says. "The asshole is a treasure chest with many precious secrets locked inside. What I'm showing you is just a mere taste, a few of my simplest tricks. Look at how hard your dick is now, and how your balls are pulled up tight. These are some of the signals a man's body gives when he is about to shoot his load. It is important that you be aware of this, so that you can stop in time. A truly skilled cocksucker can draw a man to the brink of shooting many times before finally triggering his orgasm." Gregor smiles. "But because time is limited, I must bring the first part of your lesson to a close. Observe me closely."

Gregor swallows my dick again. He teases the shaft with his tongue as a second finger joins the first in my asshole. He bends his knuckles. The jolt of pleasure is sharp and unexpected, and I give a long, trailing groan. Gregor increases the pace of his cocksucking; my dick glistens with his saliva, and I can feel my load being pulled from my balls with each ascent of his mouth.

Suddenly he presses a finger hard between my balls as the fingers of his other hand push all the way into my asshole. I cry out and my body shudders. Gregor jacks me off as I shoot, pulse after pulse of my thick load splattering his face. When the last drop has squirted, I sink into a chair. I look at Gregor with dazed, astonished eyes. Gregor regards me calmly, my load dripping down his cheek.

The room is silent except for the sound of the fountain in the courtyard outside. Gregor wipes his face with a towel. "Well, Nikos," he says. "Did you learn anything?"

"I...I had no idea..." I swallow. "You are most skillful, Gregor."

Gregor laughs. "These are skills I can teach you, Nikos. If you're willing to learn."

"Does that mean that I can work here?" My heart beats hard inside my chest.

Gregor nods. "Yes, I think so. In fact, I want you to start tonight." He kisses me on the mouth. "But we have much work to do before then." He leans back, his hard dick laying against his belly. "I want you to suck my cock again, Nikos. Using the techniques that I've just showed you. And when you've mastered those, there are others you'll need to learn."

I lean forward and run my tongue up Gregor's dick. Outside, the fountain splashes softly.

The room where the clients meet us is large and sparsely furnished: a bar at one end, couches and chairs scattered along the walls and in alcoves. The windows are open to the night air, and a breeze stirs through, scented faintly with jasmine. Other young men, my fellow "escorts", sit by the bar or lean casually against the wall, their poses polished and confident. I feel clumsy beside them. The clients sit at the bar or on the sofas, some talking to escorts, some alone. Gregor has dressed me simply, in tight black slacks and a white cotton shirt with an open collar. "You don't need any embellishments, Nikos," he said when he gave me the clothes. "Your looks speak for themselves."

With a soft drink in my hand—none of the escorts are allowed alcohol—I stand next to the fireplace, my eyes fixed on the flagstone floor. I glance up to see Gregor talking to a man who arrived alone a few minutes before. Gregor is smiling and nodding. They both glance back at me; Gregor motions for me to join them.

"Nikos," he says. "I'd like you to meet Mr. Waverly. Mr. Waverly is an American visiting Athens for a few days."

I look at him, curious. I have never been this close to an American before, much less spoken to one. Mr. Waverly is in his mid-30s, tall, at least half a head taller than me, with dark-blond hair and the beefy body of an ex-football player. "Hello, Mr. Waverly," I say, stumbling over the foreign name.

He holds out his hand. "Call me Jack." I shake, looking directly into his face. His eyes are gray and very bold. They scan down my body and back to my face. "I've heard about your place. From friends." He winks. "I thought it would be an exciting experience to come here." His Greek, though heavily accented, is surprisingly good.

Gregor smiles politely. "Nikos is new to us, Mr. Waverly. He would be most happy to attend to your pleasure." He pauses discreetly. "However, if you wish someone more experienced..." Jack shakes his head. "No," he says, smiling. "That won't be necessary." I see the excitement in his eyes. And the hunger. "I think Nikos and I will get along just fine." He turns to Gregor. "I'm ready." I am slightly shocked at this abrupt transaction.

Gregor leads us upstairs. On the stairway, Jack throws an arm around my shoulders, like we've just finished a soccer match and are off to the showers. Do all Americans behave like this, I wonder. Gregor escorts us to a room and closes the door without a word. Jack and I look at each other. He grins. "Nervous?"

"Yes. Does it show?"

Jack laughs. "A little. Around the eyes. You look like you might bolt."

"I'm sorry," I say. "Please forgive my inexperience."

Jack laughs again. "Don't apologize. It's the ultimate fantasy. To fuck a virgin in a whorehouse." He kisses me on the mouth, his tongue pushing between my lips. It is so strange to feel whiskers against my face. "Let's get naked," he says.

We quickly strip. Jack's body is solid and massive, the chest hairless, the skin of his torso as red as his face. His cock is red, too, and it lays half hard against his thigh, leaking precum. I stare.

"Do you like it?"

I look up. He's grinning, his eyes are gleaming. "I have never seen a circumcised cock before," I say. "Why do you Americans do it?" Jack shrugs. "Beats the hell out of me." His eyes take in my body, slowly, gratefully. "Christ, you're beautiful," he says softly. He reaches over and squeezes my dick, stroking the foreskin up and down the shaft. His hand is large and callused, the knuckles sprouting blond hairs, the fingernails broad and square. I am still surprised at having a man's hand wrapped around my dick. Even Kyria hardly touches it. But it excites me, and my dick stirs and stiffens to full hardness. Jack's eyes meet mine, and the hunger in them is naked and urgent. I have seen that look on men's faces in Hydros when a particularly beautiful woman walks by. How strange I should inspire the same look.

Jack runs his tongue over his lips. "Nikos, I don't know what is allowed here. Sweet Jesus, I would love to fuck your ass! May I?"

Gregor spent the afternoon introducing me to his collection of dildos, preparing me for such a question. From the nightstand drawer I pull out a condom package and jar of grease. I hand them to Jack, smiling, saying nothing. Jack laughs, wraps his arms around me, and we topple onto the bed.

I start to roll over, but Jack stops me. "I want to look at your face when I fuck you," Jack says. "I want to see your expression every time I shove my dick up your ass." He bends down and we kiss again, our mouths working hard against each other. I feel his fingers, slippery with grease, burrow into my ass crack and push against my bunghole. Two fingers slide in, moving up and down, and I tremble with the sensation. I spread my legs wider and push my hips up. Jack pulls his fingers out and slowly, inch by inch, slides his dick up my ass. His eyes lock onto mine. "Yeah, Nikos," he murmurs. "Relax, let it happen, that's it, baby, accept it." I stare back, my eyes wide, my mouth open, panting. Gregor's dildos were nothing like this, nothing like a living cock. I groan softly.

Jack pulls out slowly, until the head of his cock is barely inside my asshole, before he thrusts it in, all the way, burying his cock deep inside. I cry out and pull his head down, kissing him fiercely, biting his lips. Jack pumps his hips, his dick sliding in and out of my ass, his balls slamming against me, his broad chest squirming against mine. For an instant he keeps his dick full up my ass and grinds his hips against mine. I groan louder. Jack wraps his hand around my hard dick and beats me off, his strokes in synch with the plowing he's giving me.

We roll over, Jack on his back now, me straddling him from above. My hands slide up and down his torso, kneading the flesh, grabbing it, feeling the hardness of a man's body, so different from a woman's, so exciting in its difference. Jack varies his strokes, sometimes long and deep, sometimes fucking me with quick, sharp thrusts. His eyes burn into mine, his lips are pulled back into a snarl. He strikes my chest with his fist, his fingers opening into a long caress that slides down my torso. His other grease-smeared hand works up and down my dick, each stroke pulling me closer to the point of release. I run my fingers through his hair and then close them into fists, shaking his head from side to side. When I was younger, before I married Kyria, I would get drunk and fight men in the local tavern. Sex with Jack feels like one of those brawls, the same excitement, the pitting of one man's strength against another, only this time, instead of pain, we try to weaken each other with the pleasure.

Jack whimpers. He pulls out and then thrusts, deep up my ass. His body trembles beneath me, and he cries out. His muscles convulse under my hands, he arches his back, his dick throbs inside me as he squirts his load into the condom up my ass. He thrashes violently and I clamp my thighs together, holding on until he collapses onto the bed, still panting.

He looks at me with dazed eyes. His hand is still stroking my cock, sliding up and down the shaft. "How close are you to coming, Nikos?" he asks.

"Keep doing what you're doing," I gasp. "I'm almost there." And indeed, it takes just a few more strokes of Jack's hand to trigger my own orgasm. I groan as my load arcs into the air, splashing Jack's face, coating it with thick, creamy ooze. Jack accepts it with closed eyes and open mouth. I collapse besides him, and he slides his arm under me, pulling me close. We lie in silence, until we hear Gregor's discreet knock, telling Jack he has five more minutes.

Jack sighs. Then he laughs lightly. He gets up and starts dressing. "I come into Athens regularly for business, Nikos. Maybe I can see you again next time I'm here."

I smile. "All right."

On his way out, Jack kisses me lightly and slips a tip into my hand. I glance down and see that it's more than I would make at a week of fishing. I put the money in the pocket of my slacks, still lying crumpled on the floor. Gregor comes in shortly afterwards.

"Well?" he asks, his eyebrows raised.

"Gregor, I would be happy to continue working for you. Or rather for Stavros. Just as long as I can visit my family on Hydros regularly."

Gregor grins. "Mr. Waverly left very satisfied. I think we can work something out, Nikos." He raises his eyebrows. "Can you take on another client tonight? It's busy downstairs."

I nod. "I think so. Just give me a few minutes alone, first, all right?"

Gregor winks and leaves the room, closing the door.

I lie in the bed, staring at the ceiling. How strange life is, I think. After a few minutes I sit up and start getting dressed to join the party down below.

UnSafe Cyber

Dan Taulapapa McMullin

(for Patrick Scully & Eric Gupton's PosiTV)

BustAGut: wassup?
BitterFaerie739: My dick.
BustAGut: yum yum!
BitterFaerie739: Stats?
BustAGut: 5 8", 200 lbs., 40, asian, avg/cut
BitterFaerie739: Sorry, too old and too heavy.

WOOF: Hey, stud.
BustAGut: what s up?
WOOF: My dick. What s your stats?
BustAGut: 6 1", 180, 32, blond, hung and uncut. wanna meet?
WOOF: Ya!
BustAGut: What do you like to do?
WOOF: Everything.
BustAGut: What do you look like?

WOOF: Read my profile.
BustAGut: oh, ya. brb.

AuntieMaim: Bust! Hey how s it going?
BustAGut: oh, fine, i m kinda busy
AuntieMaim: Jeez, guy, it was great meating you the other day. You re so nice to be with...exotic!
BustAGut: be right back, i have to let the dog out

BustAGut: hey, stud. hot profile! i wanna suck that big dick!
WOOF: So, can I fuck your face?
BustAGut: ya......fuck me.....feed me.....
BustAGut: i wanna let my head hang over the edge of the bed....and see you stand there......fucking yr hot cock down my throat
WOOF: Every fucking inch down your throat, you like that?
BustAGut: ya...! i want it all....
WOOF: All the way in, all the way out, slowly at first..
BustAGut: fuck my throat.....just ease back every once in a while to let me breathe......then fuck it with deep strokes again
WOOF: YES, LET ME FEEL YOUR TONGUE LICKING IT ALL UP, LET ME SEE YOUR EYES LOOKING UP AT ME AS I FUCK YOUR FACE

BustAGut: oh ya man! i go wild looking up at you as i take you down all the way and my tongue licks yr entire cok...

BustAGut: hey! just downloaded yr pic! i want you, man!

WOOF: I M CUMMIN DOWN YOUR THROAT, EAT THAT SPUNK, BITCH, SWALLOW IT!

BustAGut: yeth!! yeth!! glrmmglrmmmm.........

WOOF: ARGHARGHHHARGHHHHARGHHHHHHHH!!

WOOF: I like it wet and wild.

BustAGut: what a pic, that s a nice ass you ve got

WOOF: It s not too hairy for ya, is it?

BustAGut: how can it be too hairy?

WOOF: Suck that hole, ya punk.

BustAGut: mmmm, ya, licking up and down yr shaft, over yr balls, up and down yr crack, tonguin ya deep, fingering that hot wet hole

WOOF: Oh ya open me up baby.

BustAGut: oh ya open up for me babe, open that wet hole up for daddy

WOOF: Ohhhhh fuck me daddy, give me that hot dick!

BustAGut: oh ya sliding my big dick between yr cheeks....slipping it against yr waiting hole....are ya ready for me? are ya open?

WOOF: FUCK ME WITH THAT HOT COCK NOW!

BustAGut: ya! thats what i like to

hear! jammin the head up yr hole, fucking the whole thick length deep up yr bung, allll the way deep in ya, shovin my fingers with my dick, jammin my balls up yr wide open fuck hole ya hot white bitch!!!

SweetCakes: Girrrlllfriend you wont believe what just happened to me!
BustAGut: girlina what? ya know i m busy with the mens just now
SweetCakes: I won a door prize at Neiman Marcus, can you believe it? Their one millionth customer! It s a fur coat of course my husband says I should burn it.
BustAGut: let me call you girl, brb

WOOF: YA I WANT IT ALL, CUM UP MY BUTT YA HOT FUCK!
BustAGut: oh yaaa i cant stop it now cummin up yr hot hole, ooooooo ya baby
WOOF: Ohhh ya man I can feel your load shooting up in me.
BustAGut: oooo ya....oo...oo...yr so hot, still shooting loads up yr ass.
WOOF: Man, my ass is all tore up. You know how to give a good fuck. I can feel the cum dribblin out my hole, down my thighs.
BustAGut: i like to give as good as i get. yr hot!

WOOF: I have a confession.
BustAGut: what?
WOOF: I m not Italian like it says in my profile.
BustAGut: i have a confession too...i m not a real blond
WOOF: That s ok.
BustAGut: that ain t all.
WOOF: What? Don t worry you can tell me.
BustAGut: i ve got HIV
WOOF: WHAT?!
BustAGut: i ve got HIV i said
WOOF: NOW YOU TELL ME!? After what we just did? What did you think you were DOING?!
BustAGut: well, i got carried away
WOOF: I can t BELIEVE this. We had unsafe sex and you didn t tell me. You fucking bitch! I oughta slap you up!
BustAGut: well

[message: WOOF currently logged off.]

BustAGut: jeez, sometimes ya can t get a nut anywhere...

See Dick Deconstruct

Ian Phillips

I'm thinking of an image. It's from one of those stories where Our Father throws Lucifer out of the house for good. I can't remember which.

Maybe Faust.

Maybe Paradise Lost. It doesn't matter. All I remember really is the image.

It's of the future Satan sitting among us and forever looking back towards the one place he would never be able to return. Which leads to more stories. Ones where, to soften the pain of remembrance, The Fallen One tries to stick it to The Man by sticking it to one of The Man's favorites.

Think Job. Think Jesus.

In a way, this is one of those stories.

Sort of.

I have no idea what The Man or any other god thinks about my little boy. But I do know that before we met he was fast becoming a darling of the Academé. Not just any old university—the Academé, site of all discourse and inquiry located in that great metanarrative in the sky.

I'd seen his name several times before he told it to me that night. He'd been a contributor to various anthologies. Ones with glossy covers in garish colors drawn on a computer. Covers that promise a mondo-pomo-homo-a-go-go world within. Then you turn the page. Instead it is only a book filled with straggling bands of menacing, jibbering words from the clans Tion or Ize. Words which must wander those pages forever at war—sometimes even with their own in the same sentence. Leaving behind a field of white, strewn with participles dangling, dying.

To be honest, I don't know if it was just dumb luck or synchronicity that led me to answer his personal. And, after what I did to him our first night, he's the one who'll want to dig up Jung and ask him whom or what to thank. I merely made the most of a moment.

His personal? Something about a Queer, White Dork, this weight and that height, goatee and glasses. Has a hard spot for hairy, horny daddies. Grooves on the transgressive in theory and praxis. Then the standard blah blah blah.

I had no plans for what we'd do if things clicked. Not even after I recognized QWD's name. My inspiration came only after he offered me a cigarette.

I smiled and shook my head. His brand, not his offer, had surprised me. American Spirit. This boy had spent a lot of his time and someone's money redecorating his mind in early 1970s French cultural critique. I'd expected Gitanes. Or maybe, in the down-and-dirty spirit of Genet, that he'd have rolled his own. But no, he smoked American Spirit—filtered. He'd been out here on our brittle bit of the Rim of Fire longer than I'd thought.

He lit up. A real feat since we were sitting outside this cafe on Market Street. That shouldn't mean anything to you unless you've been to San Francisco in the summer. It was late afternoon when we put our first pints on the table. And a late summer afternoon in San Francisco means that the fog flying in over Twin Peaks uses Market Street as its landing strip.

So as gust after gust touched down, he lit up. On the third try. And, by then, he was curled so tightly around the cigarette he looked like a fetus hugging its heart.

He sucked a few times on the burning paper and then spoke. I had the masculine signifiers he wanted—bulk, a beard—or so he said. But, he added, I was smaller than the men he'd been with before. And I thought, yes, I am small; beware the small.

I know. I know. You probably don't give a shit what we said or what I look like. You only want me to describe my dick and what it did. I won't. Call me a tease, but we both know one man's dick is another man's dink is another man's dong. Besides, I'd rather give your puny little imagination a workout. So maybe I have one. Maybe I don't.

The boy and I kept talking. Through several more beers, cigarettes, a course of spring rolls and pad Thai, then along the streets and up the stairs to my apartment and down the hall to my bedroom.

We stopped beside my bed. I put one of my short, thick fingers to his lips. I stepped back. "Strip."

He beamed. Quickly, he gripped the bottom of his terrycloth shirt of many colors and yanked it over his head and down his arms. His nipples stood out on the pale skin. Two dark dots. Alternating patches of muscle and bone. All strung together by a few hairs running from his breastbone to the rim of his shorts. He knelt and unlaced his Airwalks. They'd been the color of wet sand, but in the unsteady light of the room's candles I could barely see the whites of their laces or his socks. He put them all against the wall and returned to the spot beside my bed. He unbuttoned his shorts, let them drop, stepped out of one leg and, with his foot in the other, kicked them over towards his shoes. I could forgive this smiling eagerness to please as a bit of nervous excess, but that kick smacked to me of precociousness. My suspicion was confirmed when he tried to lock eyes with me as he tugged his white cotton briefs down over his budding cock and then his thighs. He had to look down once he got to his knees. As soon as his underwear was at his ankles, he raised his back so I could get a good view of his dick. It was long and fat like an animal's snout. It flopped against his balls while he shook one, then another, foot free.

It'll do, I thought.

I looked up and met his eyes. "It's interesting how it's often the choices made with the least thought that carry the most damning consequences." He blinked. "Like your high kick. Very precious. I don't like precious." His eyes widened. "Maybe I should just send you home…." He blurted out something. The beginning of a plea. I jerked my right index finger to my lips. He swallowed a paragraph of yet-to-be-spoken words.

"What—no one's ever spoken to you in the conditional? I said 'maybe'. I said 'should'. You'll stay as long as I want you to stay. And that might even be the whole night if—if you obey my one rule: you may speak, but each sentence may have only three words; and each word may have only one syllable. Otherwise, you can jabber away at the cab driver on your way home. Agreed?" He nodded. "Are you sure you don't need me to diaper that mouth with a gag?" He shook his head so hard his balls swung from thigh to thigh.

Always the student, I thought, craving tests. Good, we'll begin with the hardest. So I decided to take a few long minutes and bind him tight with the one thing I knew he feared most—silence.

It began when my face stiffened into a stare. He smiled nervously for the first few seconds. I think it was a minute before I even blinked. By then, his lips had filled in the gash of teeth. We listened to our breathing. To the sputtering of the candles. Finally, I turned and walked out of the room. I left him alone in the squirming shadows. It would be three, maybe five, minutes more before I'd return with a wad of pink fabric tucked in my right fist.

I tossed it towards his feet. The wad fluttered up into the air and blossomed into a pair of pink silk panties, a size five women's, a snug fit even with his narrow hips. The one-petaled flower fell fast to the ground. "Put them on."

He crouched to pick them up. He fumbled trying to get the crotch going the right direction. He stepped out of one leg and turned the material around the pole of his other. The panties slipped up his calves and over his knees. Then, he had to tug slowly up along his slim thighs, over the ass I'd yet to see, and around his resistant cock. The waistband snapped at his hips and his dick was plastered against the right side of his pelvis. He looked up. Either the material chafed or he was pantomiming defiance. I didn't care.

"Take off your glasses."

He chirped. Something about no longer being able to see.

"What's to see?"

I walked up to him, pulling a strip of leather out of my back pocket. I let it hang out of my right hand, though I doubt he could see this. I got behind him and lifted it above my head, then over his. I tied it around his eyes. I stepped back in front of him. As I pressed my hands close to his eyes to adjust the blindfold, I could smell his face. It was bitter with smoke and fear. I lingered long enough for his cold skin to feel the warmth from my breath.

I moved away. "You've talked a lot today. Most of it, I enjoyed. In fact, by dinner, I felt like I was back in school. Shooting the shit at three in the morning with a paper due at ten." I paused to cross the room and return with my butterfly knife.

"I have just one question. It's about what makes a man. You seem to know. Well, you did in that article for *Homosex(e).*" He started as he realized how naked he'd become. "What was your thesis for that one? Something about 'penetration being a mode of production in the manufacturing of the masculine'?" I stopped to let his own stilted words limp over to him.

"I'm sorry. Here I am contextualizing my question and I haven't even asked it. Let me try this again. First, I'll introduce some givens, then the question." I opened my left hand. "This is a dick," I said while I pushed my palm flat against the pink panties and then his prick until each were mashed against the wall of pelvic bone. I waited for his dick to stiffen and push back. Hand and cock then began a little dance until the hand had shuffled the tip of the dickhead up and under the strangling elastic waistband. Below it, a swelling pink stem was pointing towards the ceiling.

"Then," I said as I plucked the head, nearly in full purple bloom, "to use your own terms," and I pulled flower, stalk, and the taut rim of the panty out to me as far as I could—I almost lifted him up off his feet—"there's what you called the concretized phallus." And now my right hand and its knife reached into the gap between his dick and his belly.

I turned the knife on its side and stroked the dull edge of the cold blade up the shaft, prickling with hairs and goosebumps. "Actually, anything with a point'll do." My left hand slowly let go so that only the knife held his cock and the overextended waistband in place. "So here's my question. If I took this," and I flicked my left index finger at his dickhead, as if it were a marble and this were a game. I paused to feel it thud against the warming metal. "If I took this and left you with this," I pushed the concretized phallus against the cock that was trapped on the other side by my finger, "would you still be a man?"

I waited.

The muscles of his stomach flinched, shaking the skin that rippled the air that stirred the hairs on my arm holding the knife. I hoped that this was his answer. I waited. It was.

I almost smiled. I was beginning to enjoy our date. For now I could spend the rest of it teaching him the deeper meaning of his wordless response.

I pulled the knife out in one stroke. The panties snapped his prick back in place. He gasped. He was stung but uncut. I grabbed both his hands and pulled them towards me and the bed as I jumped up onto it. I rolled off the other side still holding him. I let go and he lay across it. I took his left hand and tied it to the left post of the black metal headboard. I moved around the bed knotting and cinching his three remaining limbs to the three remaining corners.

Then I stood. Breathing deeply. I'd worked fast and was winded. I'm sure he could hear my snorts over the thudding of his own heart.

For the first time, I saw his pink ass. I jerked the waistband down and under the curves of his butt. The smooth, round, white cheeks plumped like breasts lifted by an underwire bra. I cupped them with both my palms. They grew warm. Pap. Pap. Pap. Three swift slaps to warm them more. I allowed a few moments of silence. Enough time for his ears to stop ringing. So he'd be able to hear this. I yanked the tail of my leather belt out of its buckle so hard that it creaked. Next belt and buckle slithered into my hand. The treated and tanned skin groaned as I bent it, then snapped it taut.

"You cocky little fucker. Answer me." The dead animal's hide slapped across the hide of my little live one. The echo of the clack somersaulted around the room. The candles wavered. But he said nothing. This boy who, in print, had never made his point in under 15,000 words, said nothing. I was growing quite excited as I realized there might be a spark of brilliance in him after all.

"Or maybe you can't." I began to punctuate each sentence with the end of my belt. "Not because you're too dumb." *Thwack.* "Not because you're too smart." *Thwack.* "But because you're one of those pitiable scholars who can't speak without citing someone else." *Thwack.* "Must explicate." *Thwack.* "Must legitimate." *Thwack.* "Must use the f-word." *Thwack.* "Foucault." *Thwack.* "Foucault, Foucault, Foucault." *Thwack, thwack, thwack.*

His ass was pink again. Almost roseate. I took my left hand and let my fingers survey those patches that even in this dim dark shone. "Such a hot ass," I said. I lowered my head towards it. My tongue slipped and slid over the nearly hairless skin as if it were ice. Ice that seemed cold and smooth, but my tongue grew warm against it, felt its throb. "Such a hot ass," I said again, and left the room.

The kitchen isn't far from the bedroom. A few feet. He must have heard me open the mouth of the freezer. Heard it sing its one long, cold note. Heard the spine of the ice tray crack in my hands. "Miss me?" I think he moaned some answer. "Miss this?" I dragged my tongue back along the trail left by my belt. I'm certain he was groaning when I took my tongue and pried at his crack, digging deepest near his hole. He tried to push his ass closer to my face. So trusting for one I'd thought so critical.

I lifted my head. Now, before my saliva could dry, I pressed down the melting cube. His butt muscles clenched. I retraced where the tongue, first of my belt and then of myself, had been. His whole body tensed as I pushed the cube down between his cheeks. "Such a hot ass," I whispered. I nudged the ice over his hole. It was sweating its own lube. I took my thumb and ground it into his asshole. He rolled his head over the pillow, biting at it. "Go ahead. You still have your dick. Be a man and scream." He tried to kick me off. Maybe he yelped. I dug at the decomposing ice cube with my fingernail. It plopped out. I slid it down towards his balls, leaving it to melt.

He began to twist against his ropes. All this show to shake off a shrinking chip of ice. I grabbed the scruff of his neck. Then I gave him a swift, sharp blow with the belt. He was still.

"You lied to me." I struck him again. "I've read everything you've been able to get published so far. You posited yourself over and over as a master theorist. Acted like you could demystify any obfuscation thrown your way. Like you were going to deconstruct the cosmos. Down." *Thwack.* "And down." *Thwack.* "And down." *Thwack.* "Until your praxis led to your dick. But why'd you stop there, boy." *Thwack.* "What's so fucking special about your dick?" *Thwack.* "Is it magical?" *Thwack.* "Is that where you keep your male essence?" *Thwack.* "Your fucking trans-historical male essence?" *Thwack.* My left hand pulled at his hair and shook his head while my right hand flung the belt over my back. "You fucking hypocrite." *Thwack.* "You're nothing but a fucking," *thwack*, "closeted," *thwack*, "essentialist." Mid-stroke I stopped.

The harder I had hit, the higher his ass had leapt. On the last stroke, it jumped up to meet the belt. "No," I said out loud. I wasn't going to let him take control of the scene. This was about my revenge. Not his pleasure. Not tonight. Not on our first date.

I climbed onto the bed. I sat on his butt. Even through my jeans, I could feel the warmth of his skin. I sat there a moment, like a hen on her almost-hatched egg. I sat there a little longer. Soon, I thought with instinctual certainty, soon.

I leaned over his back until I was crouched over him, my belly pushing his head deeper into the pillow. I untied the left hand, then the right. I crawled off him and the bed. I untied the left leg, then right. With both hands, I dug for the waistband that had now burrowed under the cheeks of his ass. I took the elastic and scraped it up along the skin. Before I left go, I gave a final yank and, snap, his panties were pulled up.

He began to mutter, reciting a rosary of "no's." He must have thought I'd untied him to send him home.

I tugged the ropes and the boy over to the chair and down across my legs until I felt the smooth fabric and the stiff cock slide across my right leg. I stopped when I had his dick bent over my knee just so. As if it had been scaling the outer wall of my leg and was now stuck, unable to heave the balls over.

Keeping the ropes in my left hand, my right hand was left alone to tear down his panties for the last time. I could feel the faint pulsing of his cock. It wouldn't be much longer before he wet himself. A few good slaps. So I decided to take my time. I ground my palm into the small of his back. Then I turned it on its side and started to push at that firm pink border wall. It gave a bit. A budge more. Then it recoiled, scooting my hand back to where it began.

Once more. This time I rolled my hand back onto its palm and let it curl into a fist. I plowed against the panty waist. My knuckles, like the broad lip of a shovel, tried to lift it. Instead, they pushed under the rim and over the warm earth of his ass, until all momentum was lost and my hand flattened again, this time over that long fissure venting heat from its deep hole.

It was a pleasant moment. Unexpected. I dragged my hand out to try yet again. I placed my knuckles half on skin, half on silk. The boy squirmed a bit. I felt his cock flatten against my leg. He was growing impatient, insecure. Good. I would go even slower now.

I took my knuckles and rubbed at the edge of his right hip. Several tries and I got the rim to fold over on itself. I moved my hand towards the left hip. I did the same there. Soon I had the elastic turned in and out all along the edge of his butt. Now I would knead and roll and knead and roll the panties down as if I were making a pie crust. By the time I had them tightly under the ledge of his ass, I'd left his skin stinging, throbbing even, where the elastic, like a crude lawnmower, had torn out some of the few black hairs. And, though I was pleased, I could feel that my little man's interest had waned.

"Don't fall asleep on me, boy." I slapped his cold butt hard enough that my baby had to fill his lungs with air. "Do I bore you? Afraid you'll drift off before your queer elder passes the staff along to you?" I felt his body hesitate. He actually thought of answering me. "Oh, is that it?" I yanked the ropes and his wrists to the floor. I let my voice drift back in time and up an octave. "Fuck me, daddy, sir." Possessed, I began to bounce him against my knee and whack out a beat while I said, "Yes, sir. Yes, sir. Fill me full."

I stopped. His skin shook. His cock quivered. I leaned towards his left ear and whispered hoarsely, "I will, young man, but when I'm good and ready. Do I make myself clear?"

I tugged the ropes again. His dick slid over my leg until his balls were flat against the side of it. "Huh?" I let go and he slunk back. I pulled again. "Well?" Then several more times until I knew these slow kisses between his silk and my denim must have been burning his dick. I could feel it swelling. I let him slide back and forth over my leg several more times as I kept shouting, "Do I?" The last time I didn't let go of the ropes. His cock and balls could barely teeter on the edge of my quite warm thigh.

"Now, you're going to tell me the truth. Aren't you, my queer-core kid?" I slapped his ass twice. My palm stung. "You're going to tell me just how much of a lying essentialist hypocrite you are. Aren't you?" And I began to whack at the fleshy underbellies of his cheeks. Soft fat, some muscle. I kept whacking all the while I kept shouting. "Aren't you a liar? Aren't you? Aren't you a fucking closeted essentialist? Queer theorist, your ass. You never read Judith Butler. Did you? Did you? No, you hunched under your covers with a flashlight reading Judy Grahn and diddling yourself. Didn't you? Huh? Didn't you!"

By hitting the undersides of his butt cheeks, I'd been lifting his ass with each swat, forcing him to rub his cock over and over against the hard muscle and bone in my leg, making his own body first slap his balls and then mash them against the side of my thigh, so hard and so fast that the silk and denim were close to sparking. Even if I'd wanted to stop beating on his beet-red butt, it wouldn't have mattered now. He would've kept on humping my leg like the precocious panty-wearing dog he was.

Now, for every word I would speak, I batted at him with whatever strength was left in my nearly numb hand. "I know you read Mark Thompson's *Gay Sprit* over and over and over..." A yes spilled out of his mouth. "And over and over and over..." Another yes. "Until you were weeping and clapping for fairies."

YES! He bucked forward and then rocked back on the fulcrum of my leg. It shook wildly, then he did. And did. And did. He was spewing a loud stream of yes's now.

I waited. He moaned, a low sound, while rolling from side to side. I let go of the ropes and let my left hand fumble about until it found my knife again. I passed it over to my aching right hand. In a series of jerky, sawing strokes, I cut up the left side of his panties. When I reached the waist, they sprang apart. Now I leaned forward and cut open the right side. I put the knife down and steadied the boy's butt in my hand. With my left, I reached under his panting chest and pushed him up. Next, I grabbed the soaked front of his panties and pulled. My right hand felt the back end come slithering from both sides into his crack and up the crevice towards his balls. I watched his face contort as the fabric brushed up and up his still-too-tender shaft.

I shoved his left shoulder gently. He dropped slowly to his knees, dragging his drooling dick along the denim, leaving behind a silvery streak like a snail's trails.

Once he landed on his knees, the real dumbshow began—he was bobbing up and down like a puppet with a broken string. One awkward attempt after the other to balance the weight of his body on his calves without letting them actually touch his butt. For a minute, it was amusing. Certainly more arousing than his striptease. But he kept on squirming and I grew bored. I bent sideways and fumbled along the floor. I was looking for the other thing I'd brought back with me from the kitchen. My hand patted the rug until I saw it glint in the candlelight. It was one of those tiny spoons used for cracking the boiled shell of an egg and scooping out its jiggling white insides.

I opened my left hand and dug around in the pink wad with the spoon. I slid it under a shimmering blob of cum. "Open wide." I turned towards him. Even with the blindfold, I could sense his blank stare. "Your mouth, brainiac." He hesitated, then dropped his jaw. "Here comes a little spoon for my little man. Filled with man essence. Your man essence. Eat up." I rested the spoon's cold underbelly on his lower lip. Instinct and that even crueler master, desire, made him do the rest.

"That's it. Eat up all the sacred man essence. We wouldn't want your sex to grow up without a gender, would we? No, we want your sex to have a gender," I said as I wrapped my hand around his plump cock and squeezed. "A manly gender."

I scooped out an even larger dollop. And, while he sucked down that spoonful, I smiled to myself. I was humming by the time I made him lick the still-sticky insides of his panties. And it wasn't because I knew my little man was ready to be fucked. It wasn't even because I knew, from that night on, I could have this little man as long as I wanted him. It was simply because nothing soothes the forever-broken like breaking another.

From *A Contagious Evil: The Mind of a Serial Killer*

Larry Townsend

This is the account of my friend Ralph's first nocturnal encounter with Alfred Kleinhauser. It is constructed from notes I made a couple of days after hearing it, plus a few of my own interpretations—added at a much later date, after I had come to know Ralph Humphries well enough to feel comfortable projecting some of my own conclusions into his discourse. Later on, he was much more casual in relating the stories Kleinhauser told him, and in my opinion this first exchange—purely sexual in nature—was somewhat more than it first appeared to be. The prisoner was horny, I'm sure, driven by intense desire. But he was far too clever, too calculating, merely to engage in a fleeting sex session. The seduction of his guard paved the way for other things—for a chance to engage the man in detailed and personal conversation within a relationship where it would be difficult, if not impossible, for the other to tell about the stories Kleinhauser would relate. At first, there seemed no reason for me to write down an account of Ralph's admissions. Later, I was glad I had, as it offered another bit of insight into the strange, twisted labyrinth of the serial killer's mind. Of course, the fact that both of us were half drunk when we discussed this first episode did little to enhance Ralph's recall—or my own subsequent memory when it came time to record it. At this early date, naturally, I could not anticipate the extensive, personal interaction I was to have with Kleinhauser. Thus there was not the same degree of urgency to "get it all down" as I would experience a few weeks hence. So, with that caveat, here is my recollection of Ralph's narrative, slightly reworded in conformity with my own sense of literate exposition.

Ralph's First Exchange with the Highway Stalker

I was working twelve midnight to eight A.M., so most everyone else was asleep. I took advantage of this to do some reading, and to go over my notes from class. I wasn't really violating any rules, except that I was sometimes late on my rounds; I was supposed to unlock the gate to the corridor of cells at least every half hour, and walk the length of the hallway, looking into the five occupied cubicles to make sure the inmates were all there, and all still alive. There was a big concern that someone might commit suicide, although I don't know why they should be so worried. This was Death Row, after all, and every guy here was destined for the gallows—or the needle. If he did himself in, so much the better, I thought—save the state some money. But no one dared say this in so many words, and no one wanted it to happen on his shift.

My first conversation with Kleinhauser came during my second week on the job. It was about three A.M., and I was making my sixth trip down the corridor. I had reached the end, where Kleinhauser lay in the last cell. As I was turning to go back, he whispered to me. I hadn't expected anyone to be awake, and the rasping sound made me start. "Come over here a minute," he said. He was lying on his cot, on his belly, with his head toward the bars. I knew who he was, of course, and despite my contempt for him I was still somewhat awed. He was, after all, the biggest celebrity on The Row. He was also quite good-looking—small stature, but with well-developed arms and legs, clearly visible to me as he shoved back his blanket and assumed a half-crawling pose. It was warm in the cells, so he had been sleeping in just his jockey shorts. His face was almost pretty, and his manner verged on the delicate. It was hard to believe that this harmless-appearing little guy could have been a cold-blooded serial killer. Even more puzzling was how he had been able to subdue his victims, some of whom must have been considerably larger and stronger than he was.

But I soon realized he possessed something more than physical strength. He had a way of speaking, and of looking at a guy, that made you want to believe what he was telling you. On this first occasion with me, he motioned me closer to the bars, as if he wanted to whisper some secret. I was not carrying a key to his cell, and he knew I wasn't, so I was not afraid that he might try some trick to escape. I moved near him, and he started to talk to me in that hoarse undertone, so soft it forced me to pay close attention in order not to miss anything. Thus I was within a few inches of the bars, standing slightly bent forward as he began to plead with me to "stay a while," to "help break the silence and keep him company for just a few moments."

I have to admit I was intrigued from the very beginning. There was a definite sexual aura in his manner, and as much as I wanted to break it off and walk away from him, I couldn't do it. Instead, I stood there listening to him recount his fears. He was often afraid to fall asleep, he said, because his dreams were sometimes terrible nightmares. At this first encounter, he did not describe them in any more detail, but he seemed genuinely isolated, very much in need of some human companionship. Despite my being sure he was guilty of the most bizarre and gruesome crimes—acts of depravity that were far worse than those committed by any other man on The Row—I also recognized him as far above the rest of them in intellect and education, and in his former socioeconomic status. He had been a successful stockbroker, and a couple of years before his arrest he had been written up in two major business magazines.

This was all in the past, however, and no vestige of his former lifestyle manifested itself in his present demeanor. He was a prisoner, lying nearly naked in his cell, begging his guard for a few minutes attention. As he spoke, describing the boredom and indifference of his other jailers, he slowly uncoiled his body and slipped onto the end of his cot. He was looking up at me with a strange, almost pleading expression. He was angling for something more than simple conversation. I knew this from the beginning, but I felt almost compelled to stay there. Nor can I deny the sexual urging, either. I was twenty-two, after all, at an age where lust rose easily to become a dominating, all-excusing force. Inwardly I knew what he wanted from the beginning, so when he went onto his knees on the cement floor I moved closer to the bars, allowing the front of my uniform pants to brush against them.

My motion had been an unspoken response to his invitation. The long slender fingers of his left hand slowly traced the seam of cloth along my fly, while his right slipped under the waistband of his shorts, shoving them off his narrow hips and permitting his half-risen cock to flop free, hanging in swollen tumescence, swaying slightly with the motions of his body. He pressed his lips against my groin, looking up, his dark eyes reflecting the dim overhead corridor light and seeming to glitter in the darkness. As he continued to stare at me, his fingers sliding into the enclosure of my fly and fumbling for the tab on my zipper, I had a peculiar sense of who he was, or more precisely what he'd been. I saw him as he must have appeared in his converse role…standing over the prostrate, tightly-bound form of his naked victim, hunkering down, forcing his cock between the unwilling lips.

It had been a fleeting projection in my mind, and I tried to reject it, tried to drive it away, but the very perversion he represented excited me, compelled me to stay where I was until he managed to free my cock and possess it with a really desperate passion. His heat engulfed me, and something of his pent-up lust seemed to flood all about me. My rod was enveloped in a hot, clinging moisture. I sank into it, closed my eyes and gripped the bars for support as my knees suddenly threatened to give out. He took me deep in his throat, possessed my flesh as his mind had tried to take hold of mine—or so it seemed on later reflection. For the moment it ceased to matter. He grasped me in a hungry, desperate, almost violent possession—as well he might, for I knew he'd been deprived of physical contact during his entire incarceration. However compelling the sensation may have been for me, it must have been manifold as intense for him.

As his lips and tongue worked their magic, he reached for my belt and undid the buckle, shoving everything down my legs. I tried to prevent his doing this at first, but he released my cock just long enough to whisper something about messing up my uniform. Then he slipped my leather belt from the loops in my fallen uniform pants and—without slackening his motion against my groin—slipped the body-warm band around his neck, passed the end through the buckle and forced the resulting noose into my left hand. Thus I was holding him, like a dog on a choke-chain, involuntarily assuming the role of his Master. The situation evoked a strange sensation, as you might imagine. Then, once he knew that I had a firm hold on his belt, his lips gripped even more firmly around my desperate hardness. His hands grasped my naked cheeks and played their warmth against the trembling curves. He was forcing me forward, then, making me slam my groin against his lips. I had to be hurting him, but he seemed to want this; and his motions became even more frantic when I pulled upward on his improvised leash and half choked him. His face became dark red from the constriction, but he never slackened his possession—not even when I began to gasp, warning him of my imminent climax. He was like a man possessed, which perhaps he was, but in those moments I lost any ability to consider more than the purely physical sensations that had taken hold of my body. That there might also be some danger to my soul never occurred to me, and whatever muted voices of warning might have sounded in the back of my mind were lost in the roar of lust pounding in my ears, and the enervating sensation of release echoing through my entire body.

After I'd cum, and stood gasping against the bars, he sat back on his haunches and once again looked up into my face. There was the barely discernible trace of a grin on his lips when he licked them, as if some exotic essence remained upon them. Slowly, I stooped to retrieve my belt and to pull up my fallen clothes, wondering—illogically—at his having swallowed my load. No one did this anymore, but he seemed to read my thoughts and grinned again. "I won't live long enough to worry about it," he said softly.

A few minutes later, sitting at my desk trying to read a textbook, my mind refused to focus. I kept seeing him kneeling there with my belt around his neck, naked with a pool of his own jism cooling on the cement between his knees. His expression had been indecipherable—probably a result of the many emotions he must have felt, sexual relief above all, but satisfaction as well because he had willed my participation and I had given in so easily. He must have wondered. He must have had some doubts, for I am sure that even during this initial encounter he must have been plotting his future encounters with me. His evil mind must already have been planning how he might use me, take me over—or more to the point, make me over.

He knew there was no way he might escape. No amount of connivance, even if I had been willing to risk everything for him, would ever have gotten him through the outer gate. He had to have known this, and so his scheme must have been to achieve a different goal. His freedom would come though me, nonetheless, but in a way I could never yet have imagined. So far, he had compromised me to only a minor degree. But it was a start. I was already obsessed by him, and sitting at the desk I kept recalling his image, kneeling there naked, helpless behind the bars, yet not helpless. Even then I recognized this much—that he had the power of his mind, which equated to the power of evil. Despite all other circumstances, I was afraid of him. The sudden realization startled me, and I stared blankly into the dimly-lighted passageway, through the bars that separated me from any physical danger. I saw the red button on the desk that would summon immediate assistance, but nothing could assuage my ill-defined anxiety. Alfred Kleinhauser was poised to take control of my innermost being; but I was not yet free enough of his spell to realize it.

Ralph's first encounter with Kleinhauser happened shortly after our own first meeting, and our abortive sexual encounter. However, it was several weeks before Ralph told me about it. Looking back on that period of time, I think it is possible to see some marked evidence of change in his behavior—at least in some of his attitudes. Without any forewarning, of course; this is sheer speculation. I may also be projecting hindsight as insight.

As best I can reconcile the time sequences, the jail incident took place on a Tuesday or Wednesday night. Ralph had Friday and Saturday off—a compensation for his voluntarily taking the late shift for the rest of the week. We had arranged to meet at the Black Cat, the closest thing to a leatherbar in the city, at eleven Friday. I arrived first, and was nursing my beer when Ralph pushed through the beaded draperies at the front entrance.

After the usual exchanges of pleasantries, Ralph remained silent for several minutes, as if deep in his own thoughts. Then, unexpectedly, he said: "Hey, why don't we cruise around awhile and see if we can pick up a sailor out on the highway?"

He surprised me, and I didn't answer right away, but I must have had a quizzical expression on my face, because he went on: "I did this once before with another friend of mine. We'd pick the kid up, and the passenger would shift over to the middle of the front seat, with the sailor—or Marine, if we were lucky—sitting next to the door. Then, as we're driving along the guy in the middle starts playing with the kid's leg, and if he's cool about it, he gets a blow job."

"That's not much fun for the driver," I said, forcing a little laugh, because I wasn't sure if he was serious.

"Oh, we took turns driving—switched back and forth at regular intervals, even if we didn't find any hitchhikers. And for sure, we changed places if one of us got a piece of meat in his face. Friday's a good night, too, because there are lots of guys—mostly servicemen—heading up the highway for a weekend at home, or whatever."

"You're serious."

"Sure I'm serious. It's fun. Whatta'ya say?" He glanced at his watch. "If we take off now—it's not quite eleven-thirty—we can get back here in time to catch the action in the alley after the bar closes in case we don't make out on the highway."

"Or even if we do," I added.

He looked surprised, now, in his turn. "Yeah," he agreed, grinning. "Sure."

Crazy as the idea sounded, the prospect really excited me. We used Ralph's car, because he had a big Chevy with a wide bench seat. He drove first, and when we didn't have any luck after about a half hour, he pulled over and we switched places. Thus I was driving when we found our first sailor—a handsome little guy in a white uniform, thumbing at the intersection of the highway leading west toward California.

The kid got in, putting his small zipper case on the floor between his feet. As we pulled back onto the asphalt, I could feel a slight tremor in Ralph's body, where his hip touched mine. From the corner of my eye I could see his big, blunt fingers caressing the starched surface of the young sailor's whites. The kid made no protest, actually slumped down in the seat a bit and spread his legs. Ralph had the sailor's cock in his hand about two minutes later, stroking it and playing his thumb across the head. The kid had a roaring hard-on of fairly respectable proportions, as best I could see in the uncertain light. There were no streetlights along the highway, of course, and we had the instrument panel dimmed. So it was only in the reflected glow from on-coming cars that I could catch an occasional glimpse. Then it didn't matter, because Ralph bent over the kid's crotch, and gave him a very enthusiastic blow job. There had never been a word spoken about or during the exchange. The young sailor simply leaned his head against the back of the seat with his eyes closed, enjoying the ministrations of the bigger man.

We dropped him off at a gas station/restaurant, then turned back toward town. A mile or so down the road, I stopped and changed places with Ralph. "That was a hot little number," he remarked. "I wouldn't have minded taking him for a longer ride."

I didn't question his meaning, although I have subsequently wondered exactly what he intended. We made several more passes at the more popular intersections without success, and were on the verge of returning to town when we spotted a young kid hitching at the junction of a smaller county road that led off the main highway. Ralph pulled up, the kid climbed in, and we started down the murky, completely deserted road. It was very dark, without even the glow of lights from occasional buildings along the way. There was no other traffic. Tall weeds grew on either side, interspersed with occasional planted fields or orchards. The kid had made some remark when he first got in about being lucky to catch a ride this time of night. Then he sat silently until I gathered nerve to gently lay my palm atop his thigh.

His reaction was immediate and violent. He shoved my hand away and started screaming. "Let me out! Stop the car and let me out!"

He was hysterical, and Ralph tried to calm him, telling him there wasn't anything to be afraid of. "You don't want to get dropped off here on a dark road," he suggested. "Let me take you on up to some place where there's light."

"No," screamed the kid, "No, let me out...right here! Let me out!"

Ralph pulled up on the shoulder; and the kid bolted out the door into the brush alongside the road. Ralph killed the lights and backed the car away from the spot where the kid was bumbling his way through the reeds. "Don't want him to get the license number." Ralph continued backing up for another hundred yards. Then, with the lights still off he turned the car around and we roared off into the darkness.

I was still shaken by the encounter, thinking—illogically enough—of ways the kid might be able to identify us, worried now about the repercussions if he did. Obviously, the same thoughts had occurred to Ralph, or he wouldn't have gone through his elaborate escape scenario. But the terminus of his thought patterns was very different from mine.

"We should have kept the little shit," he muttered at length. "That's the kind that'd be the most fun, strung up under a tree, stripped naked and screaming curses at you while you whipped his ass. Yeah, too bad we couldn't have just hung on to him and played him for all he was worth."

"And both end up in jail," I reminded him. "I don't even think he was of age."

Ralph shrugged. We'd reached the highway, now, and he headed us back toward town. Neither of us spoke for several miles, the blackness of night rushing past us on either side, with only an occasional set of oncoming headlights to penetrate the gloom. Then Ralph said softly, his voice pitched down and deep: "We would have had to get rid of him afterwards…no other way. Too bad. If it weren't for that—weren't for that," he sighed. "Mighta been fun."

I would emphasize once again that my time frames are tentative, although I am completely sure that Ralph had been involved in only one session with Kleinhauser at the time we went on our first nocturnal "hunt," as we came to call our cruising sessions. Whatever the source of his callous attitude toward the kid, it disturbed me—frightened me, largely because his words caused a warm sensation to envelop my crotch. In fact, the whole fantasized scene excited me despite my other negative emotions. I am quite certain that it was three weeks before I got together with Ralph Humphries again. I know this because I deliberately avoided him until I got over my fears, or at least got them under control...although I was never able to forget the intensity of my own excitement. Partially because of this I was afraid to say much about my own feelings when Ralph came by on a Friday night to share the wine that resulted in his telling of his sexual contacts with Kleinhauser. Then we didn't have any contact until the following weekend—again a Friday night—when Ralph came by to pick me up. He had called and left messages on my machine a couple of times, wanting to make the date. Finally, afraid that if I put him off too long he'd be pissed, I left a message saying I'd meet him and go on a "hunt." Interestingly enough, his perceptive abilities had seen through my charade.

"I shook you up last time we did this, didn't I?" he said lightly, as his big Chevy moved slowly into the flow of traffic on the town's main street.

"Yeah," I admitted, "You did."

He laughed softly and patted my thigh with one enormous paw. The warmth of his touch seemed to penetrate my fears, and for a moment I was unaccountably aroused. "Let's take a drive, even if we don't do anything," he said. "I got some things to tell'ya." And with that he accelerated across the intersection as the light turned green, leaving all the other traffic far behind. In those moments I wasn't sure if he intended a repeat of our previous month's quest, and in truth I was surprised at my own disappointment when he implied that maybe we wouldn't do more than ride around. I simply wasn't sure whether I wanted to try it again or not. My balls were saying yes, but in my mind there were lingering doubts.

"I gotta tell'ya about this Alfred Kleinhauser," he said at length. "The guy's really gettin' to me."

"Aren't they getting ready to execute him? I think I read something in the...."

"He goes in about six-seven weeks," Ralph told me, "and it looks like it's for sure this time, 'cause they've exhausted all his appeals, and the governor's already said he won't grant clemency."

"Sonbitch doesn't deserve it. Clemency, indeed! How many kids do you suppose he killed?" Then, thinking back to my interview with him: "I know it has to be a lot, even though they only convicted him for one."

"That's right. You met him when you did that interview, so you know what he's like. The thing is—" Ralph was suddenly silent, thoughtful.

"Whatta you mean?"

"Well, see—the shrinks and the profilers—they figure for sure he did eighteen, and they suspect he might have done a few more somewheres else—maybe in another state. But—" He sighed almost painfully. "He actually did a lot more than that—in a lot of different places, and he's fuckin' scared!"

For a moment I wondered if I'd understood him; then he want on. "See, Alfred's gotten into some of this religious stuff, but all on his own, not with some priest or minister. They got a lotta that kind'a books in the prison library, more than any other subject, and he's read 'em all. He's scared shitless that the spirits of the kids he's killed are all waiting for him on the other side. He's scared to die—has been for a long time. But now that it's getting closer, he's started having really bad nightmares, until sometimes he's afraid to sleep."

"Are you still...?"

"Oh yeah, I think it's the only thing that keeps him going. He can't wait until I come to make my three o'clock rounds. We agreed never to try it earlier, just in case someone's still awake. But he's waiting for me at three—kneeling naked just inside the bars. As soon as I get close enough, he reaches out and gets my zipper down—sucks on my joint like a baby on a nipple. He doesn't stop when he takes my load, either. He hangs in there until I get soft, although sometimes...well, sometimes I get hard all over again and he takes the second one, too. When that happens, I can hear him making almost sobbing sounds, and he hangs onto my ass-cheeks like he's afraid I'll run away. Then, after he's taken all I have to give him, he starts talking to me. Honest, Hal, I wish I could'a recorded it all. You never heard such a story in your life!"

"You think he's telling you the truth? Not making it up to impress you?"

"Oh, I don't think so. Some'a the things he's said—oh, man! And it's funny, ya know; he keeps telling me these stories, then he stops and he whispers something like, 'You won't repeat this, will you?'—like he thinks I got a direct line to the local yellow sheet. And I haven't told anyone," he added quickly, "...no one but you. But I can't keep it all to myself."

A crazy thought was already churning in my mind, but I didn't mention it until we'd driven for another fifteen or twenty minutes. Despite my earlier reservations I knew I wanted to speak with Alfred Kleinhauser again. My first interview had been a fluke—or so I thought. I realize now that he had actually wanted to spend some time with a young, reasonably good-looking man. That was his reason for selecting me from the long list of professionals and others with far more experience. Whether my being gay had anything to do with it, I don't know. Later, when I listened to his dreadful confessions of terror and torment, I became convinced that the sexual preferences of his victims were immaterial to him. Still, at that earlier time, he might have felt that a gay man was going to be easier to talk with, possibly be more sympathetic. I'm still not completely sure.

My one interview with him in his cell at the county jail, just after his trial, had been three years before. I knew he had not given another interview since. He had declined every offer that had come his way; and there had been plenty, from many different sources. But knowing that I was Ralph's friend, I hoped he might agree to see me again, although at that point I had no way to know what he really felt about my first story. I had tried to take a neutral stance, not to condemn him in my rhetoric; his own deeds did that without my having to express any sense of my own horror or disgust. His statements at the time had not been admissions of guilt, anyway. He had waxed philosophical and gone into discussions of historical sex crimes. He had denied his own guilt, even for the murder that he'd been convicted of—not really going into any details, just skirting the subject in passing.

But when I wrote up the interview I had not speculated on the crimes for which he had not been convicted, and I hoped that this might stand me in good enough stead that Ralph could talk him into seeing me again.

After a short discussion of how it might be done, Ralph agreed it was worth a shot. "If nothing else," he told me, "I'd like someone else to hear some of what he's told me. If I repeated it, they'd lock me up as some kind of a nut."

We were on the highway by this time, and Ralph spotted the white uniform before our headlights hit him, at which point Ralph resolved my previous indecision. "Here's your score," he said jovially, and began to slow the car.

Ralph Humphries, despite his normally slap-happy, bubbling good humor, had been more affected by Kleinhauser than I could possibly have imagined at this point in time. In a display of uncharacteristic efficiency he set the machinery in motion for my journalistic coup. Without telling me he was going to do it, he got the prisoner's consent to my interviewing him; then he arranged for me to meet his uncle, Sean McIntyre, warden of the prison. When the secretary called to make an appointment, she caught me completely off guard. "…eleven tomorrow morning, then," she said.

"I'll be there," I told her. And in truth, this marked a decided change in my whole life. When I called my editor to tell him what was going on, I think he danced a mental jig and offered me all the time I needed, took me off any other assignments and authorized a very generous expense account—in case I needed to spend some money getting things for Kleinhauser, or "whatever." He wasn't sure how this sort of thing worked, but however much it took of my time and his money he wanted me to go for it. "Stop by the office tomorrow or the next day, and we'll draw up a proper contract," he said. "I'd been hoping you'd get a chance to go back and talk to this guy again, but I'd been afraid to ask after the things you told me—about how you felt and all, from before."

Everyone, it seemed, was delighted I was going to interview Kleinhauser for a second time—everyone except Yours Truly. I still had some reservations—and if I'd had any idea at all of what I was getting into, I'd have had a lot more.

So I went to see Warden McIntyre at eleven the next morning. His office was on the top floor of the main prison building, perched so that he could see the prison yard from one side of his suite, a vista of foothills and distant mountains from the other. He wore a dark suit of some heavy, stiff-looking material. His tie was scrunched into a tight little knot, and he gave an overall impression of being slightly rumpled. He was almost completely bald, with a shiny dome that reminded me of some B-movie alien. I almost expected to see the veins stand out and vibrate as he spoke.

He motioned me to a chair facing his desk and settled his bulky body into a high-backed swivel behind it. He regarded me narrowly at first, through rimless glasses set atop his rather substantial nose. Then he grinned and his whole aspect changed from grim authoritarian to benevolent parent. "Ralph tells me that Kleinhauser is willing to talk to you again," he began.

I nodded. "That's what he says."

"Well, that's good news and bad news," he told me. "I've had every kind of professional, semi-professional, screwball, and government official you can imagine, all coming here trying to get this asshole to see them. He's refused every damned one. They all desperately want to question him, and he's finally assented to your doing it. That's the good news."

He laughed at my confused expression, at which point his secretary knocked on the door and entered with a tray of coffee and Danish. McIntyre let her put things down and leave before he resumed his interrupted discourse. Pouring a mug of coffee for me, he continued: "The bad news is that just as soon as the vultures discover that you're doing an interview they're going to be all over you—and all over me." He held up one beefy paw in something approaching a peace gesture. "No, that's okay. I can handle them, and once you start I think I can keep them off you—here in the prison, anyway. But I'm just going to let you go ahead without special notice to the Board of Prisons, and without asking permission. If I simply let you go ahead it'll be *fait accompli* before they find out. If I ask, someone's apt to say no, or stall for somebody else to make a decision. I have a feeling there is a lot to be said, and not much time to say it."

"Won't the…the higher-ups know I'm coming in to see him as soon as I start?"

"Not necessarily. The prisoner has suggested that you interview him during Ralph's shift, and if you do that you won't be seen by so many people. I won't try to hide it, but I'll simply include it as an item in my routine reports. Someone will probably pick up on it, although I suspect that more often than not these reams of paper get filed without anyone reading them. In any event, as long as I inform the 'higher-ups' as you call them, my ass is covered. I can't help it if no one bothers to read my reports."

"Do you think it's going to be that important to very many people?"

"Oh hell, yes! Professional jealousy if nothing else, is going to be a factor. And then there are some very legitimate concerns among the mental health people—and the FBI profilers—and the state law enforcement officials. Yeah, once they tumble to what you're doing, you're going to get a lot of attention, maybe some flack, certainly lots of requests to find out one thing or another.

"But I'll shield you as best I can, 'cause I frankly believe you got the best chance of finding out exactly what this fucker's done, and maybe get some hints as to why he done it. I assume you got it all squared away with your newspaper?"

"Oh, sure. They're…."

"Happy as a pig in shit," laughed the warden. "Well, good luck, kid. I hope you can get the real story from our reluctant dragon. And…well, I hope you're prepared for what you're going to hear."

A New Harrington and Oxblood Rules, o.k. (Jumping the Broom)

Lawrence Ytzhak Braithwaite

to Stephen Beachy

So he met him...

You should haf seen hem he waz a beauty/ areal lil'darlin. Maybe jus a lil over me n I'm not too tall myself. He was the phuk, man.

I get to see him mostly at this pub house on Saturdayz. He jus sits by himself n readz. A book, hez got always spread eagle, pulled apart by booth of his wide finger tipped handz. His face pulled into it. I wnt to go over n talk to him alot, but I never got the nerve.

I'd knew I'd treat him nice though. I see him alot walking around. He waz rude for sure. He had the wickedest crew. They a' yite, I guess, he'd put it, but I could bust a nut over him iz wot I say. I alwayz could for Sparker. It waz amazing. Why doez he look at me like that, real sweet, wit thouz big blk eyez n that smoik?

Sometimez like last week. I look over n he'z jus look'n at me. He noddeds n I still cant go over or say some'n. I figures it would be stoopid, the thingz I would say. He'z got a cast on: wh' appen.

But that turndout to be stoopid too. He was nize, it turndout.

HEZ MY BOY.

It's fun to see all of it go down. It waz whatelse could have happened wit thoze two—wot goes on inside…

I saw him the otha day wit that gutter skin, Philly, sittin ontop of a newsbox on the street. Jus starin down at me. He'z too rude. He'z too stackt—what a neck, such a smile. He'z got lips, up close, that could stop a speeding train. So soft, I could use my mouth n finger to meet it and leave my fist to hold my heart.

He couldn't even come over and say hi wotsup. How long could I keep readin that phukkin book. I need to get a res somtime n that would be jus look'n o'r to him. He waz caught, sometimz, starin back, but he don't come over or say hi…nah no, that don't cop no shit. I n'er made a move beside an eyeball mov'n over hiz direction once n'while. Then I get my face bek btwn the pages. Sometimes I'm jus starin at the words n his face appears n I kiss it. His lips r wide n soft. I figure he'd turn hiz hed roun n smile 'cauze he'z cute like that, I figure. But I'd still have hiz neck to breath against n here myself escape from his mouth.

Strange though, all it took waz Killer Peppey movin tablez over one day…

Speak to me…

-Yush, anyone sitting here, buddy-
-Nah, nah ga hed-
-Nice stingy…-
-You never seen one before-
-Don't be crass-
-It's my middle name-
-Kiss my neck, yush, you are a smartass, aren't ya-
-Ruffy, sameting, if you're asking dumb questions-
-Like you guyz keep a low profile. I'm not impressed. Anyone sitting here? Guess not, yush-

Killer Peppey went to grab the seat and walk.
-What do ya think-

Sparker shows the lining of his harry.
-It's gud 'rite. They were never slaves-
-You're not a stewart-
-I'm not a slave-
-They owned them-
-Before you head on back to Babylon: I'm Sparker…don't be an jackass—mek a fren tadeh-

Killer n me got askt to Sparker'z families place for a 4th Bar B'Q. All he could say iz:
-Any pork-
-No…no-
-…ah, gud-
I remember when he took hiz hand. He shook it. One hand (soft) held Killer'n thother reached over n touched the top, enclosing the whole thing. Killer figured he liked him then—guy-bye wazn wot Sparker waz sayin…

Most people, especially dEVILZ, find out that they're that way or whatever and they start to strut down the runway like they've been condemned or sometin; dementia dry humpin in syncro. They got this look like they smellin somethin alla the time.

Momz, Popz, Brothaz, Sistaz, Auntiez and Volk—hiz crew'z there. Everybodiez turned out tuff, Top Skins, ruff, well sharp. Bandalous all—Sparker'z crew, not hiz family. A Volkishe gath-er'n. It waz a family wit southern roots: Afro-Am Southern Aristocracy—could trace their tree of life past slavery 'n I think to the 1st guy who built a hut—n everyone wontz to know 'bout Killer n me.

They talk...
They talk...
I nod'z n chew'z

This boss shit doesn't happen alot—cool nights. There'z great reggae playin—The Upsetters. Sparker'z at the tablez. You don't get to hear this shit usually: true bashment tunes. He just cranks the shit. Nobody stays down. Killer'z right in the middle of things dancin, having a blast—which iz rare—seeing *him* smile, painless.

Whatz soopir cool. The Horde are here. They're Sparker'z crew. They're the snorkiest—even more than the dumbdumz. You got Mark and then Re:Mark—there are 2 baldiez named Mark so...go figure, Bomb, Cyco, Kreeg, Zombie (he's the drummer for The Finger Mashers—you got to talk to this dude if you want to find out why he'z called Zombie) and Roadkill—they found him outside a Warzone/Templars show passed out, spread, ready on his back on the street. He waz pissed to highheaven. He kept mumbling something like "you can't trow me out." They just watched for a while deciding what to do, laughing, asking him if he wanted a beer, seeing if a truck wouldn't swerve in time...adoption waz the only option. Turns out he came from Virginia—so they were doing him a favor by telling him he could hang wit them and not go back.

They grabbed the table where Killer 'n me waz sitting. They gave greeting.

-Philly, how'z our bredda. Cheerz, Killer, let us get you a beer- and these guys know how to get to your heart. Wot can I say?

-Yeah so you don't like girlz-

I thot they were laying in to me, maybe Killer, but that wouldn't be bright moving wit Killer. But, nah, it waz something to do wit Zombie.

-Nah, nah, nah, I didn't say that. I said, that putting that goil in Jonny Quest waz a stupid idea. Jonny Quest iz a guy show and goilz don't fit. Just look what they did to Hadji...-

Cyco asks hin.

-Wot did they do to Hadji? He's bigger that's all-
-Nah, he'z not phukin bigger. He'z...-
-He went through puberty-
-I don't want to talk about that-
-Puberty-
-This iz Jonny Quest-
-He'z a cartoon-
-Yeah-
-Who went through puberty...-
-Nah...-
-...wit Hadji-
-Hey, look, Hadji iz a computer geek now and the goil, she'z-phukin annoying-
-That'z Race's lil girl-
-Yeah, ok, how did Race get a kid-
-You don't know this Zombie-
-You're talking about sex again and this iz Jonny Quest-
-Did you ever think...like the idea came across your mind maybe, that Race Bannon waz having it off with Doc Quest-
—No! and i read a book about that stuff and homos can't breed-
I wazn't going to say something to that 'cauze it came from Zombie. But Re:Mark said something about turkey basters?

Sparker'z brotha, Malik, got up on the picnic table n threw hiz plate aside n pointed at me n holler'd:
-I AM MY BROTHAZ KEEPER-
Sparker sayz:
-Hey great, he likes you-
I stared at hem wit my gud eye n it jus came closer to hiz face n I saw Sparker in hiz face in his eyez n you could see it n all there eyez n faces. I don't got somthin like Sparker.

I waz having a time trying to make sense of what Zombie talking about. He tried to read a book again, the otherday.

-It sayz, that people are homos because they're weaker than normal people and so they weren't meant to reproduce-
-But, ah, there's artificial insemination-
-Yeah-
-...and a guy could get hard pump it up and pump it out into anything. Doesn't mean he favored it-
-OK-
-...and then there'z turkey basters-
-Yeah, I think my sister did that-

Why wouldn't Malik like me. I'm Philly Blunt—I'm cool.

He waz a stranger but I'm not a strange land. I wonted to invite him back to the squat.
-Come to my house Sparker-
-I don't know...it's cool. All kinds of shit happening here-
-After...-
-...-
-What'er you starin at-
-Come with -
...oh Killer, I could crash into those lips. You should get out of my head, sweetness...but Sparker'z got that smile wit a gap btwn hiz teeth, alla the light got caught wit hiz eyez...
-Comeon Sparker-

...Killer touched his belly w/hiz finger...

Sparker in my armz. I donna if he'd let me touch him that much.

They way off over on the other side of the yard. Nobody matterz at this point, I guess. They, they're gone—the phuks.

W/ Sparker in my armz//he feelz so warm.

Killer's lips could rst ontop of neck forever and...

They didn't damage anyone or the other'z skin too much. It's still all, smooth, some zipperz from life and stuff.

He patz and strokes me.
On our mat.
We got a candle going. It's not non too safe to do that/but we like it better than electric. Edison's too expensive anyway. Sparker'z got the patent on this one.
I hear Killer breathe and it's slow and peace like.
The first time Sparker let me see him naked, I was all sunk down mushy/in my heart.
The first time I saw Killer take my hands, I pulled him wide open and rubbed my head against hiz chest.

I don't do too much/cause I figure he's like me.
In bed, I get scared people are going to hurt me. So I don't bother too much w/ that stuff.

My hed bobz with his chest.
He smiles inside.
I/myself/laugh to sleep and wakeup the same.

There'z no damage to Killer'z skin. No internal damagez. Not much I would'n have the strength to handle.

Wit my one gud eye I like to look at the drawingz Sparker putz up on the wallz. They take place here and in his head. He draws the Rudies n Moonstomper's he meets at places—clubz n pubz, on the street—alot of the crew. I think that onez of Killer the otha of me. Me I draw him in my mind. They say Blk absorbz all light. So mine iz filled wit them all. It's better than television or moviez. He'z got stuff of me. He doez nice pictures. He waz in art class, before now, and they said he wazn't goin nowhere. He used spray paint and crayon n gouche n wordz n wordz. His subjexs were hansum, pretty enuff to be on that tree of life of hiz n hiz familiez', guyz absorb'n light.

Wit thoze 2…it'z all thrash.

I keep Killer on the top of my head and start to dream.
Done ciphering/
In an act of imagination/
I thanked my new venture for all the joy/
pain/
hurt n fun it would bring forth
   …and summoned up a holocaust/
and thoughts of
Nikki.

Wright,
Hemphill,
Toots,
The Upsetters—in total praise—
and my
and my
and our
crepuscular heart(s) exploded
infinitesimally
explode in honour.

He'z (M)fren like the sparks in my hed.
I try to get back to Sparker…
To grab hem close…
…fear beats me to the punch;
   -Yush, com'ere, letz get some sleep. I'm phukin bagged—

About the Authors

Belasco/James Tucker is author and illustrator of a number of popular chapbooks of erotic Black gay male art, including the Belasco comics series *Lust for Sale*, *Confessions*, *Enter Lewd* and *Nassssty* and the collections *What Gran'maw Saw*, *Nuthin' But Feet & Azz*, *Li'l Big Dick in Midnight B-Ballin'* and *Boo: Down 'n Dirty*. His work has been re-printed in the *Meatmen* series (Leyland Publications). He lives in Los Angeles.

Lawrence Ytzhak Braithwaite is the author of *Wigger*, a novel cited in Brian Bouldrey's *Best American Gay Fiction 1996*, and of the short story "Bloodland," cited by Bouldrey in 1997. His work is an intense and twisted insight into abuse, the world of the ultra-violent, and the brutal life of being young, male, and neither right nor left of any center. His new manuscript, *Ratz are Nice*, concerns Rudeboys, Skinheads and a dodgy dude—Huck Finn meets Oliver Twist to the crooked Oi and Reggae beat. He lives in Victoria, B.C.

Jim Coughenour is a cartoonist and writer. He is the author of *Instant Noir: Savage Tales for Short Attentions* and the creator of Daimonix greeting cards (www.daimonix.com). He's been a denizen of the Castro since 1991.

Jameson Currier is author of the 1998 novel *Where the Rainbow Ends* and of an earlier short story collection *Dancing On the Moon*. His fiction has appeared in the anthologies *Men on Men 5*, *Best American Gay Fiction 3*, *Certain Voices*, *Ex-Lover Weird Shit*, *Man of My Dreams*, *All the Ways Home*, *Men at Work*, *The Unmade Bed*, *Men Seeking Men* and all four editions of *Best Gay Erotica*. He lives in New York City.

Grigoris Daskalogrigorakis was born in Crete, grew up in the Rocky Mountains, lived for a time in Manhattan, and now teaches in Los Angeles, where he sees a lot of movies, and thinks about them, and talks about them. His friends call him Greg, spelled Ggreggg.

Jeff Kirby is an artist, performance artist, activist and educator in Toronto whose work includes *Cock & Soul* and *Drunk on Cock*; his stories appear in *Queeries*, *Quickies*, *Queer View Mirror* and *Stallions & Other Studs*. More recently he's worked on a chapbook, *Joe*, and a novel, *Head Cleaner*.

Michael Lassell is a Lambda Literary Award-winning poet whose fiction, verse, and essays have appeared in scores of literary journals, newspapers, magazines, anthologies, and textbooks. His most recent book is *A Flame for the Touch that Matters* (Painted Leaf Press, 1998). Among the books he's edited are *Men Seeking Men: Adventures in Gay Personals* (Painted Leaf Press, 1998) and *Two Hearts Desire: Gay Couples on Their Love* (with Lawrence Schimel, St. Martin's Press, 1997). His erotic writing has appeared in such books as *Flesh and the Word*, *Best Gay Erotica*, *The*

Mammoth Book of Gay Erotica, The Badboy Book of Erotic Poetry, Wanderlust, Quickies, and *Queer View Mirror*. He lives in New York City.

Dan Taulapapa McMullin is a Samoan playwright living in San Francisco. His work has been produced at the 1996 New Zealand International Arts Festival, the 1996 Pacific Festival of Arts in Samoa, Soho Rep in New York City (1995) and Theatre Mu in Minneapolis (1997). His erotic fiction appears in *Queer PAPI Porn: Gay Asian Erotica* (Cleis Press).

Poet and fiction writer **Kelly McQuain** recently won the Philadelphia City Paper Poetry Award. His fiction appeared in *Best Gay Erotica 1997, The Philadelphia Inquirer Magazine, The James White Review, Wilma Loves Betty, Kansas Quarterly/Arkansas Review* and *Best American Erotica 1999*. "Blueboy," published in the first issue of *The Harrington Gay Men's Fiction Quarterly*, is part of a short story collection called *The Truth of Boys*. McQuain's nonfiction has appeared in *The Journal of Gay, Lesbian and Bisexual Identity, Generation Q, Art & Understanding* and the *Philadelphia Gay News*. He teaches writing in Philadelphia and can be reached at kmcquain@ccp.cc.pa.us.

Ian Phillips is a queer little fellow who lives with many others of his kind in San Francisco. His fiction has appeared in *Cuir Underground, Re/Porn* and Pat Califia and Drew Campbell's anthology, *Bitch Goddess* (Greenery Press). He always reads and sometimes answers email addressed to lanrah@aol.com.

Andy Quan has lived in Vancouver, Toronto, Denmark, Ecuador, Belgium and most recently London. His short fiction and poetry appears in Canadian, American and British publications. He can be reached at andyq@unforgettable.com.

Kirk Read grew up in Virginia and is the former editor *of Our Own Community Press.* His monthly column appears in LGBT papers all over the place. His poems and short stories have appeared in *Genre*, *Christopher Street*, and a heapload of dubiously-named 'zines and websites. He lives in San Francisco now ("I've always wanted to put that line at the end of a bio!") and can be reached at kirkread@aol.com.

This is **Simon Sheppard's** third appearance in the *Best Gay Erotica* series. His work has also been published in dozens of other anthologies, including *Best American Erotica 1997*, *Brothers of the Night*, *Quickies*, *Midsummer Night's Dream* and the Lambda Literary Award-winning *Bending the Landscape.*

horehound stillpoint's most hardcore poetry can be found in *Poetry Nation* and in *Sex Spoken Here*. He is currently finishing his first play, *The Queerest Thing on Earth.*

Larry Townsend first achieved international acclaim for his *Leatherman's Handbook*, originally published in 1972. More recently, he has published the major hardcover *Czar!: A Novel of Ivan the Terrible.* He is a graduate of UCLA, did graduate work in clinical and industrial psychology, and through the 1970s was a leader in the Southern California gay rights movement. He currently lives in West Hollywood with his friend of thirty-five years, and a massive Doberman pinchser and a wily Abyssinian cat.

Bob Vickery is a regular contributor to *Advocate Men Magazine* and has edited two anthologies of stories, *Cock Tales* (Leyland Publications) and *Skin Deep* (Masquerade). His stories appear in Susie Bright's *Best American Erotica 1997*, *Friction*, *Queer Dharma: Voices of Gay Buddhists*, *Up All Hours* and *Guilty Pleasure*, among others. He can ususally be found pounding on his laptop in a neighborhood Haight-Ashbury cafe.

About the Editors

Felice Picano is the author of nineteen books, among them the classic thriller *The Lure*, *The New Joy of Gay Sex* and the international bestseller *Like People in History*, winner of the Ferro-Grumley Award and the *Gay Times* of England Award. His latest volume of admired memoirs, *A House on the Ocean, A House on the Bay* was the third in a row of his books nominated for Lambda Literary Awards. Picano was a member of the legendary Violet Quill Club, deemed founders of present-day gay literature. He started the first East Coast gay publishing company, Seahorse Press, in 1977 and co-founded Gay Presses of New York in 1981. As editor-in-chief for twelve years, he helped launch the careers of a number of writers. Picano was among the founders of The Publishing Triangle, and is now Southern California liason for its Book Aids program. He writes for *the San Francisco Examiner, Harvard Gay & Lesbian Review* and *Lambda Book Report*. In 1998 he published *Looking Glass Lives* (Alyson) and *The Book of Lies* (Little, Brown/Abacus, England). He lives in Los Angeles.

Richard Labonté is general manager of A Different Light Bookstores in New York, West Hollywood, and San Francisco, and lives mainly in SF with Asa the cranky but beloved man and Percy the bumptious but adorable dog. This is the third *Best Gay Erotica* volume he has edited; he also writes book reviews for a number of low-paying (and no-paying) but deserving publications, including *Feminist Bookstore News*, *Frontlines*, *Lambda Book Report*, *Curve* and *Q San Francisco*. He is a coordinator of A Different Light Bookstore's annual Readers & Writers literary conference, and has also scheduled gay programming for the annual San Francisco Bay Area Book Festival for eight years.

Turn the page for more great books from Cleis Press...

More Books from Cleis Press...

DEBUT LITERATURE

The Little School: Tales of Disappearance and Survival , second edition, by Alicia Partnoy. ISBN: 1-57344-029-9 14.95 paper.

Marianne Faithfull's Cigarette: Poems by Gerry Gomez Pearlberg. ISBN: 1-57344-034-5 12.95 paper

Memory Mambo by Achy Obejas. Lambda Literary Award Winner. ISBN: 1-57344-017-5 12.95 paper.

Queer Dog: Homo Pup Poetry, edited by Gerry Gomez Pearlberg. ISBN: 1-57344-071-X. 12.95. paper.

We Came All The Way from Cuba So You Could Dress Like This?: Stories by Achy Obejas. Lambda Literary Award Nominee. ISBN: 0-939416-93-X 10.95 paper.

Seeing Dell by Carol Guess ISBN: 1-57344-023-X 12.95 paper.

MYSTERIES

Dirty Weekend: A Novel of Revenge by Helen Zahavi. ISBN: 0-939416-85-9 10.95 paper.

The Woman Who Knew Too Much: A Cordelia Morgan Mystery by B. Reese Johnson. ISBN: 1-57344-045-0. 12.95 paper.

VAMPIRES & HORROR

Brothers of the Night: Gay Vampire Stories edited by Michael Rowe and Thomas S. Roche. ISBN: 1-57344-025-6 14.95 paper.

Dark Angels: Lesbian Vampire Stories, edited by Pam Keesey. Lambda Literary Award Nominee. ISBN 1-7344-014-0 10.95 paper.

Daughters of Darkness: Lesbian Vampire Stories, second edition, edited by Pam Keesey. ISBN: 1-57344-076-0 14.95 paper.

Vamps: An Illustrtated History of the Femme Fatale by Pam Keesey. ISBN: 1-57344-026-4 21.95.

Sons of Darkness: Tales of Men, Blood and Immortality, edited by Michael Rowe and Thomas S. Roche. Lambda Literary Award Nominee. ISBN: 1-57344-059-0 12.95 paper.

Women Who Run with the Werewolves: Tales of Blood, Lust and Metamorphosis, edited by Pam Keesey. Lambda Literary Award Nominee. ISBN: 1-57344-057-4 12.95 paper.

Sexual Politics

Forbidden Passages: Writings Banned in Canada, introductions by Pat Califia and Janine Fuller. Lambda Literary Award Winner. ISBN: 1-57344-019-1 14.95 paper.

Public Sex: The Culture of Radical Sex by Pat Califia. ISBN: 0-939416-89-1 12.95 paper.

Real Live Nude Girl: Chronicles of Sex-Positive Culture by Carol Queen. ISBN: 1-57344-073-6. 14.95 paper.

Sex Work: Writings by Women in the Sex Industry, second edition, edited by Frédérique Delacoste and Priscilla Alexander. ISBN: 1-57344-042-6. 19.95 paper.

Susie Bright's Sexual Reality: A Virtual Sex World Reader by Susie Bright. ISBN: 0-939416-59-X 9.95 paper.

Susie Bright's Sexwise by Susie Bright.
ISBN: 1-57344-002-7
10.95 paper.

Susie Sexpert's Lesbian Sex World, second edition, by Susie Bright.
ISBN: 1-57344-077-9.
14.95 paper.

GENDER TRANSGRESSION

Body Alchemy: Transsexual Portraits
by Loren Cameron. Lambda Literary Award Winner.
ISBN: 1-57344-062-0
24.95 paper.

Dagger: On Butch Women, edited by Roxxie, Lily Burana, Linnea Due.
ISBN: 0-939416-82-4
14.95 paper.

I Am My Own Woman: The Outlaw Life of Charlotte von Mahlsdorf,
translated by Jean Hollander.
ISBN: 1-57344-010-8
12.95 paper.

PoMoSexuals: Challenging Assumptions about Gender and Sexuality
edited by Carol Queen and Lawrence Schimel. Preface by Kate Bornstein.
ISBN: 1-57344-074-4
14.95 paper.

Sex Changes: The Politics of Transgenderism
by Pat Califia
ISBN: 1-57344-072-8
16.95 paper.

Switch Hitters: Lesbians Write Gay Male Erotica and Gay Men Write Lesbian Erotica,
edited by Carol Queen and Lawrence Schimel.
ISBN: 1-57344-021-3
12.95 paper.

LESBIAN AND GAY STUDIES

Case of The Good For Nothing Girlfriend: A Nancy Clue Mystery,
2nd edition,
by Mabel Maney.
0-939416-91-3. 14.95

The Case of the Not-So-Nice Nurse
by Mabel Maney. Lambda Literary Award Nominee.
ISBN: 0-939416-76-X 9.95 paper.

Chasing the American Dyke Dream: Homestrectch
edited by Susan Fox Rogers.
ISBN: 1-57344-036-1
14.95 paper.

A Fragile Union: New & Selected Writings
by Joan Nestle.
1-57344-040-X 14.95

Nancy Clue and the Hardly Boys in *A Ghost in the Closet*
by Mabel Maney. Lambda Literary Award Nominee.
ISBN: 1-57344-012-4
10.95 paper.

Different Daughters: A Book by Mothers of Lesbians,
second edition, edited by Louise Rafkin.
ISBN: 1-57344-050-7
12.95 paper.

A Lesbian Love Advisor
by Celeste West.
ISBN: 0-939416-26-3
9.95 paper.

On the Rails: A Memoir,
second edition,
by Linda Niemann. Introduction by Leslie Marmon Silko.
ISBN: 1-57344-064-7.
14.95 paper.

SEX GUIDES

Good Sex: Real Stories from Real People,
second edition,
by Julia Hutton.
ISBN: 1-57344-000-0
14.95 paper.

The New Good Vibrations Guide to Sex: Tips and techniques from America's favorite sex-toy store,
second edition,
by Cathy Winks and Anne Semans.
ISBN: 1-57344-069-8
21.95 paper.

The Ultimate Guide to Anal Sex for Women
by Tristan Taormino.
ISBN: 1-57344-028-0
14.95 paper.